BB ⭐

B. Milne.

Suto ⊗

ST. MAR S

whisp. I S

HEARTH OF FIRE

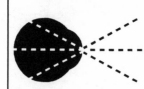

This Large Print Book carries the
Seal of Approval of N.A.V.H.

SEATTLE, BOOK 5

HEARTH OF FIRE

COLLEEN L. REECE

THORNDIKE PRESS
A part of Gale, Cengage Learning

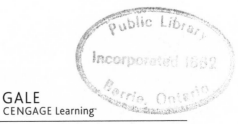

GALE
CENGAGE Learning™

Detroit • New York • San Francisco • New Haven, Conn • Waterville, Maine • London

GALE
CENGAGE Learning™

LIBRARY OF CONGRESS CATALOGING-IN-PUBLICATION DATA

Reece, Colleen L.
  Hearth of fire / by Colleen L. Reece.
    p. cm. — (Seattle ; bk. 5) (Thorndike Press large print Christian romance)
  ISBN-13: 978-1-4104-1177-8 (hardcover : alk. paper)
  ISBN-10: 1-4104-1177-X (hardcover : alk. paper)
    1. Nurses—Washington (State)—Seattle—Fiction. 2. Large type books. I. Title.
PS3568.E3646H43 2009
813'.54—dc22   2008052965

Published in 2009 by arrangement with Barbour Publishing, Inc.

Printed in the United States of America
1 2 3 4 5 6 7 13 12 11 10 09

HEARTH OF FIRE

CHAPTER 1

Thy word is a lamp unto my feet, and a
light unto my path.
PSALM 119:105

Patti Thompson leaned against the soft
green corridor wall and stared at the inscription on the hospital director's open door.
Comfort swept into her deeply troubled
mind, the same comfort the words had
brought so many times since she first saw
the inscription. Fresh from nurses' training,
heart beating with hope and anticipation at
becoming part of Seattle's unique Shepherd
of Love Hospital, the brand new RN
promptly adopted the verse as her talisman.
From that moment on, Patti never passed
the open door without stopping to read and
marvel.

How long ago that first day seemed! Patti
closed her eyes. Had she really once been
that naive, dreaming girl? A young nurse

with stars in her eyes, out to change the world even if she had to do it alone? She mentally compared herself as she was now to the shadowy image. Traces of the girl remained, but the hesitant woman who lingered in the mural-lined corridor sometimes wondered where the eager young nurse had gone. Waves of weariness washed over Patti as she continued her comparison. Both girl and woman stood five-feet, five-inches tall, weighing approximately one hundred and twenty pounds. Both had soft blond hair and blue eyes that reflected every changing mood.

Patti's face twisted. The eyes that had gazed back at her from the staff rest room on the Outpatient floor a few minutes ago bore mute witness to what a few short years could do. So did the set lips of the nurse wearing a pale green pantsuit. Suffering and disillusionment had dimmed far too much of her sparkle and stolen her Count-of-Monte-Cristo "The world is mine!" feeling that formerly characterized Patti Thompson.

Should I go forward, or retreat? Patti wondered. For a terrifying moment she felt as though she stood on the brink of a precipice. Unseen hands clutched at her, pulling her back to safety while a hidden force she was too tired to fight beckoned. *Lord, what's wrong with me?* she frantically prayed.

Her terror slowly receded, leaving her drained.

"I'm in no condition to make a decision now," Patti murmured. Realization brought relief. She turned and took the first step of the long walk back to Outpatient. The second step came easier. So did the third. By the time Patti reached her destination, the discipline required during grueling training and magnified by several years of hard but satisfying work had kicked in. She had long since learned to lay aside her own concerns in the interest of those for whom she cared. Now that knowledge served her well. A quick prayer for strength squared Patti's shoulders and brought her head up. She forced a smile that should pass inspection and briskly approached the cluttered nursing station desk.

"Anything else I can do before going off duty?"

"Thanks, but everything's under control. I really appreciate your delaying your break until now," her supervisor said. "Oh, your cowboy admirer called. Said you usually stopped by to see him after you're through here. He wondered if you were coming today. I asked if you should call him. He said not to bother and added, 'I reckon she'll come if I wait a spell.' "

Patti's low spirits rose a notch. "Don't make fun of Mr. Davis. He's a real dear, the two-legged kind. I love hearing his stories about the western Montana cattle ranch he used to own." She blinked. "It just about broke his heart when his health began to fail and he had to sell out."

The supervisor looked thoughtful. "Doesn't Mr. Davis have a son or son-in-law or someone who could have taken over for him?"

Patti shook her head until her blond curls danced. "No. He and his wife were married almost fifty years, but they never had children." She thought of the first time she had seen the white-haired, weathered rancher. He had been on his way back to Montana from transacting some business in Portland when a sharp attack brought him to Shepherd of Love. He admitted he'd experienced similar bouts before, but didn't "pay much mind to them." After the usual range of pre-operative tests, the doctors advised removing his gallbladder. The patient's reaction became legendary among hospital personnel. Never before had anyone responded by agreeing doctors should "get rid of the ornery critter as soon as possible."

"The chances are also slim anyone will again," Patti had remarked after laughing.

Dan Davis bonded with his nurse at that first meeting. In spite of his pain, he whispered to Patti, "You look like my Sarah when you smile."

"I'm glad," she told him, immediately liking the uncomplaining old man.

The procedure went beautifully, but Mr. Davis had a bad reaction to the pain medication. Dizzy and vomiting, he was in no condition to be discharged that day. The hospital admitted him as a regular patient. When they learned he had no one to care for him after he was discharged, they moved him to Transitional Care. They planned to keep him until he regained enough strength to look after himself.

"Mighty nice of you folks to keep an old codger like me," Mr. Davis told Patti when she stopped by. "Some hospitals chomp at the bit, wantin' to throw a feller out soon as he can get outta bed. How come you don't?"

"Shepherd of Love isn't dependent on anyone but God for its financing," Patti quietly told him. "Because of that, we can make exceptions they can't."

"How's that?" His eyes opened wide with interest.

Patti quickly sketched in the story of

wealthy Nicholas Fairchild, the strong Christian man who believed God wanted him to build a hospital different from all others in Seattle. Shepherd of Love, named for Christ — its real founder — did not rely on government grants, with their regulations and restrictions. Time normally consumed by fund-raisers and pleas for money was spent in prayer. When other dedicated Christians heard the story behind the hospital that leading Seattle residents predicted could never be built, they quietly furnished the necessary finances without fanfare or public recognition.

The combination of fine Christian medical personnel and prayer meetings before every shift brought results that soon earned the respect of other superb hospitals such as Harborview, Swedish, Providence, and the University of Washington's Medical Center. Shepherd of Love wisely shifted patients needing more specialized care than they could offer to the appropriate hospitals. This policy created excellent working relationships.

Now Patti told her supervisor, "Mr. Davis once asked me if I could use a log cabin near Kalispell. Evidently he still owns one. Don't look so shocked. It wasn't a proposal, although we get those, too."

"Grateful patient reaction." The older nurse sounded skeptical. "Don't start packing! Extravagant promises are typical, but they never come to anything."

Her laugh did wonders for her starchy personality. "If I'd collected all the property and money patients promised to leave me in their wills and the like, I wouldn't be here."

Patti allowed herself a moment to ask curiously, "Where would you be?"

"On a cruise, maybe? Or gloating in a mansion with a view of Puget Sound where I could just sit and stare." The supervisor laughed again. "Run along to your cowboy, Thompson. Or should I say, get along, little doggie?"

Patti giggled. "Not doggie. *Dogie,* as in a motherless calf in a range herd."

"How come you know so much about range herds?" the other nurse retorted.

"*I* was raised on Zane Grey and Louis L'Amour western novels," Patti loftily told her. "Sorry you were so educationally deprived."

"Scat!" The supervisor made a shooing motion, although the corners of her stern mouth twitched.

Patti left Outpatient, her heart lighter than it had been for days. Childhood memories kept time with her steady footsteps. Her father had been a Western history nut. He taught his daughter to appreciate an era they would never experience except through books or movies.

A small smile curled Patti's lips and warmed her heart. The bittersweet memory of her family's first long driving trip returned. Somewhere in Montana, they had swung over a hill late one afternoon. A solitary horse and rider stood etched against the spectacular Big Sky sunset.

Patti's childish heart had pounded until it felt like it would burst from her breast. All the hero figures she had only read of in books and seen in movies came alive.

"Oh, boy, a cowboy!" she had squealed.

The dark figure raised one arm, removed the wide hat Patti knew must be a Stetson, and waved toward the car's occupants. She waved back until their car rounded a bend and her first real, live cowboy vanished from her sight.

Patti's thoughts trooped ahead. Her feet unconsciously slowed. She had been so young and impressionable at age twelve! After devouring Zane Grey's novel *The Border Legion,* she had carefully packed a small bag. She kept it with her while reading in a favorite tree near their rural home.

The comb and brush, toothbrush, red scarf, and other items matched those the heroine Joan had with her when kidnapped by bandits. Should Patti also be taken, she'd be prepared. She refused to consider the fact that bandits on horseback hadn't been seen in the vicinity for at least one hundred years!

"Thank God I never was kidnapped," she fervently whispered. Yet the old desire to one day live on a cattle ranch still lurked in a locked chamber of Patti's heart. Perhaps she could visit a dude ranch someday. She shook her head. *No. Far better to keep her childish illusions than attempt to fulfill a dream and end up disappointed.*

The corners of her mouth turned down. Depression returned with a vengeance. The discovery a few months earlier that handsome Dr. Bart Keppler was a phony and cared nothing for her was disappointment enough to last her for a long, long time. So were the changes that had come to the hospital.

Patti sighed. "Lord, I'm glad my special nurse friends all married such great guys, but when is my turn coming?" She ticked them off on her fingers. "Jonica Carr. Lindsey Best. Nancy Galbraith. Even Shina Ito just deserted me." She made a face.

"Sorry, God. I don't really mean deserted. I still see my friends both off and on duty. It's just that I'm beginning to feel like the last leaf on the tree."

Patti thought of the newcomers to the hospital and the staff residence hall where she lived. Other nurses had moved into the rooms formerly occupied by her special friends. Patti felt old enough at times to be their grandmother. *At 25?* an inner voice scoffed. *Who are you trying to kid?*

She couldn't help grinning, but April and Allison Andrews did make her feel old. The ink on the identical twins' hard-won certification was barely dry. Their enthusiasm reminded Patti of her own transition from student to employee. Regret filled her. *How could she have let someone like the pseudo Dr. Keppler rob her of the excitement, the on-tiptoe thrill of challenge to her skills each new patient brought?*

"Forgive me, please, God," she repentantly whispered. Patti immediately felt better. A real smile replaced the forced one. She stepped into a large and pleasant room. Off to the side and away from the few other patients present, Mr. Davis sat gazing out the windows toward glistening, wave-topped Puget Sound. His gnarled hands lay idle in his lap. They reminded Patti of the story of

16

the "Praying Hands" painting. Albrecht Dürer had immortalized the toil-worn hands of a friend who sacrificed his own dream of becoming a great painter for the sake of the younger artist Dürer.

What stories Mr. Davis's hands could tell if they could speak! Patti wondered. *How many newborn calves and foals had they helped into this world? How often had they stroked a beloved wife's hair as it turned from sunny gold to silver? Did the fingers itch to swing a lasso, to tighten the reins and curb a wild mustang? Did the farseeing eyes look beyond the distant horizon to a place where Sarah, the beloved, waited the coming of the man who lingered a few steps behind?*

Patti felt choked up. Seeing Dan Davis in this unguarded moment offered poignant insight into what love and marriage could and should be. Two, no, three against the world, for the old cowboy had shared how God had always been head of the Davis household. She swallowed the obstruction in her throat and said, "I hear you were asking whether I'd come see you. Oh, ye of little faith."

Mr. Davis gave a guilty start and turned his head. Faded blue eyes set deep in squint and laugh lines focused on her. Their faraway expression changed to a mischievous sparkle. A chuckle started at the toes of his slippers and rumbled through his deep chest, becoming a range-sized laugh.

"That's tellin' me." He cocked his head to one side. "I reckon anyone who looks so almighty fetchin' is worth waitin' for." Approval shone in his time-worn face. "That pale green color reminds me of the willows along the creek when spring starts openin' the leaf buds after a long, hard Montana winter."

"Thanks. You're quite a poet," Patti accused.

Innocence shone clear as a mountain lake on a cloudless day. "The good Lord gave me eyes to see, didn't He?" Dan Davis pointed at her barren ring finger. "How come no one's lassoed you yet?"

Patti gave a mock sigh and clasped her hands over her heart in the best fair maiden tradition. "Alas, my friend. The men I know can't even ride a horse, let alone throw a lasso."

His hearty laugh showed how much he appreciated her response. "Too bad you didn't live when and where I did. Every cowpoke for miles around would have cluttered up the front stoop."

"The way you did with your wife?" Patti teased.

The old cowboy snorted. "Not so you'd notice! I took me one look when Sarah Mc-Clelland came to teach school and she did the same. We didn't waste much time in gettin' hitched. Stayed in harness for nigh onto fifty years."

Patti pulled a chair close to his and wistfully said, "I took a look once and thought someone was right for me. He wasn't. He turned out to be horrible. Now I —" She stared at her capable fingers.

"Feelin' a bit gun-shy about tryin' again, ain't you? Sort of questionin' your own judgment?" Mr. Davis asked. "Not that it's my business, but I've got big, listenin' ears if you want to spill anything. I also am a good hand at keepin' my lip buttoned. Always was. Sarah used to say tellin' me secrets was safer than storin' gold in a bank vault." His beguiling smile displayed strong white teeth. "If I were a guessin' man, I'd say you've got someone who wants to come courtin'. We used to call it sparkin' when I was young."

Patti considered. She really did want to talk with someone, but not anyone from the hospital. That's why she had backed off instead of going into the director's office earlier. Dan Davis would go return to Montana soon. They would probably ex-

19

change a few letters, but as he said, confiding in him would be safe. The desire to share prompted her to say, "I want the kind of marriage you had, Mr. Davis." She looked appealingly into his eyes. "I'd like to think that fifty or more years from now, someone would remember me and look the way you do when you speak about your Sarah."

"It's the only kind of marriage worth havin'," he told her. "She'd have done the same." He fell quiet, then fixed a stern gaze on Patti. "I ain't sayin' we never had our differences. Sarah and I were too spunky to always agree! It's just that we loved each other and God so much, it warmed our home and kept it from bein' a hearth of fire."

"Hearth of fire?" Patti looked at him in wonderment. "I don't understand."

"Most folks don't. Folks today don't pay much mind to the prophet Zechariah. They should. In chapter 12, verse 6, he brings the word of the Lord, sayin': 'In that day will I make the governors of Judah like an hearth of fire among the wood, and like a torch of fire in a sheaf; and they shall devour all the people round about, on the right hand and on the left: and Jerusalem shall be inhabited again in her own place, even in Jerusalem.' "

Puzzled, Patti asked, "What's that have to do with love and marriage?"

"Everything." Dan Davis glanced out the window again. When he spoke, Patti had the feeling his spirit had traveled far. "I've seen a heap of so-called love in my day. There's the demandin', self-seekin' kind that treats folks terrible and thinks sayin' 'I love you' will make everything right. It's a passionate, ragin' flame, destroyin' whatever's unlucky enough to be in its path, like wildfire on the prairie, or a forest fire in the mountains."

He turned back to his companion. "Don't be fooled into thinkin' this kind of love can be tamed," he warned. "It's excitin' while it lasts, but it won't last. When love thinks more about gettin' than givin', it's the wrong kind. It makes a hearth of fire that burns out and becomes nothin' but ashes."

Patti sat silent. What a store of wisdom this simple, range-dwelling man possessed! Her throat burned from unshed tears flowing from her still-bruised heart. Except for the grace of God, she could have married Dr. Bart Keppler and been sentenced to a hearth of fire, instead of a home filled with radiant, enduring love.

"Sarah and I loved each other 'bout as much as anyone could," her newfound

21

friend shared. "I can't remember a day I didn't urge my horse a little faster on the way home, no matter how tired we both were. Seein' the light Sarah always put in the window, knowin' she'd meet me at the door, face all shiny and glad, kind of took away the tiredness." His tone altered. "The first night after the funeral, I came in off the range hatin' to face a cold, dark house."

Patti felt his pain. She instinctively reached out and clasped his worn hand.

Mr. Davis smiled. "Don't be feelin' sorry for me. Cookie had lit a fire and the lamp, then sneaked back to the cookhouse. We never talked about it, but Cookie kept it up until the ranch sold and he and the hands moved on."

"I'm so glad!" Patti cried.

"So was I." The quiet reply said it all. Presently Dan Davis continued. "A feller havin' trouble with his wife asked me once how Sarah and I kept lovin' each other after all those years. I told him through hard times and good, we just kept feelin' thankful the good Lord brought us together.

" 'What did you do to find happiness?' he asked."

The joyous, rumbling laugh came. "I up and told the galoot Sarah and I were so busy makin' sure the other one was happy, it

22

couldn't help spillin' over onto us. Love may make the world go round, but unselfishness and carin' more about a husband or wife than you do about yourself keeps a marriage strong and healthy." He leaned forward and looked Patti straight in the eye. "Don't you ever get hitched 'nless you feel that way *and so does he.*" Mr. Davis leaned back and looked sheepish. "See what happens when you get me started? I climb on a soapbox and start preachin' at you!"

"I loved your sermon," Patti reassured him.

"Good. Are you ready to tell me about the young buck who's trailin' you?" His eyes twinkled until he looked like an oversized elf.

She glanced at the clock. "Not now. My goodness, it's time for supper and I need to change out of my uniform. Thanks for letting me cry on your shoulder."

He chuckled. "Swappin' stories is always good for a body. See you tomorrow?"

Patti thought he sounded a little anxious. "Sure. Same time, same place, if you're still here. Did the doctor say when you were being discharged?"

"Naw. He knows I ain't in a hurry. Grub's not too bad, either." Dan Davis produced a hollow, obviously fake cough. "Maybe they'll let me stick around a little longer."

"Don't count on it." Patti gave his shoulders a quick hug. "Hospitals are for sick people, not frauds like you." She slipped away with his rowdy laugh ringing in her ears and his little sermon on marriage echoing in her heart.

CHAPTER 2

A few minutes after nurse Patti Thompson's heart-stirring talk with Dan Davis, the petite blond nurse surveyed her quarters in the staff residence hall from the depths of a pillowed couch. Off-white walls, a deep blue rug, and matching draperies highlighted the small, tastefully furnished suite. Located at the far end of the leg of the T-shaped building, a large window on the west offered a spectacular view of white-capped Puget Sound in all its capricious moods. Screened windows in the kitchenette and bath overlooked manicured lawns, bright with early summer flowers and a wealth of shrubs and evergreen trees.

"I'm glad I changed locations," Patti decided. "The green suite holds too many memories of rooming with Lindsey." A reminiscent smile touched her lips. Red-haired Lindsey Best had mothered, scolded, and corrected Patti's grammar before becoming Mrs. "Chaplain Terence O'Shea," as her friends now called her.

Lindsey still did in the limited time they had together. So did Shina Ito Hyde. Patti sighed. "I've always relied heavily on my friends," she told God in the informal way she often talked with Him. "Probably too much. No more. It's time to stop being a clinging vine. That kind of woman went out of style with bustles and hoop skirts. Wonder how I would have fitted in back then?" The mischievous part of her recently suppressed by troubles took wings and soared. Patti sprang from the couch. She spread wide the full skirt of the flower print dress she'd donned after her shower. Knees bent in a deep curtsy, she fluttered her lashes in a belle-of-the-ball imitation and simpered, "My goodness, are those flowers really for little ol' me?"

The ringing of the phone destroyed pose and mood. Patti raced to answer, remembering to drop her Southern accent just in time.

"Hello?" she caroled.

Charles Bradley's amused voice sounded in her ear. "Well, aren't you happy!"

Suddenly she was, gloriously so. She felt rich color pour into her cheeks. "Would you rather have me otherwise?" She almost added "kind sir" but thought better of it.

26

Doing so meant having to explain her silliness, and she didn't know the handsome blond pilot well enough to risk having him think her foolish. *At least not yet,* her heart impudently added.

"I'll take you any way I can get you," he drawled.

His boldness snatched at her breath. "Careful," she said. "Breaches of promise have been started for less than that."

"So let's talk it over at dinner. You haven't eaten yet, have you?"

She hesitated. Last-minute dates never had appealed to her. On the other hand, Charles Bradley did.

Was the man a mind reader? Patti wondered when he said, "Sorry I couldn't call sooner. I just got in from a charter flight. I can pick you up in an hour, if you're free. How about Italian food? The restaurant Cucina! Cucina! is always good."

"Great. I'm starving." Patti loved his low laugh, although it held a note of smug satisfaction that brought a tiny frown when he told her he'd see her soon.

Her sense of fairness rushed to his defense. A man as attractive as Charles must have a hundred girls after him, yet from what she could see, he remained singularly unspoiled. Perhaps she had been mistaken.

27

"Wish I could talk it over with Lindsey or Shina," Patti wistfully said, then straightened her shoulders. "Good grief, Patti," she scolded herself. "You're leaning again, exactly what you vowed not to do! Forget it. Anyone would think you were a high school freshman waiting for her first date." Her no-nonsense reproach brought a rueful grin to her face, but did nothing toward slowing down the unruly heart turning somersaults beneath her colorful dress.

Few men of Patti's wide acquaintance topped Charles Bradley when it came to looks. The trim, five-feet, ten-inch pilot had a smile that didn't quit, blue eyes and blond hair so closely matched to Patti's they could have passed for brother and sister. Patti secretly felt glad they were not.

"What a handsome couple," a woman whispered when the hostess ushered them to the table Charles had managed to reserve. Patti smiled to herself. Her escort's dark blue shirt, matching pants, and carefully selected tie set off the tanned skin that showed signs of recent contact with soap, water, and a razor. Charles walked with head back and shoulders up, as if he owned the restaurant. "A glass of wine before dinner?" the waiter asked after seating them.

Patti shook her head. "Just water, please."

Her heart plunged when Charles hesitated. Earlier dates hadn't required a stand concerning liquor. Patti abhorred drinking of any kind. She knew what it could lead to only too well.

"I'll have coffee," Charles decided. "I think we're ready to order." As soon as their attendant left, the thirtyish pilot leaned back in his chair. "Will it surprise you to learn I couldn't wait to get in today, on the chance you might be free?"

Patti felt herself redden. She didn't answer.

He laughed. "I believe in the direct approach. If things go my way — and they usually do — someday you are going to put on a white dress, instead of that delectable one you're wearing tonight. I'll be waiting for you when you walk down the center aisle of a church, Miss Patricia Thompson."

It took all Patti's control to keep from gaping. She knew her eyes burned like headlights in a Seattle fog, but she finally managed to choke out, "My, my, we're taking a lot for granted, aren't we?"

"You sound like the nurse who took care of me when I had my tonsils out," he mocked. "Everything was 'we,' as in 'how are we feeling?' " A curious glint sent shivers down Patti's spine when he repeated, "I told you I believe in the direct approach. Relax. I wanted to give you fair warning, but I don't expect an answer." He laughed confidently. "Until at least our next date."

The waiter returned with Charles's coffee before Patti could reply, but his biding-my-time expression showed he meant every word of his unexpected proposal. *Not a proposal,* Patti hastily reminded herself. It was more a statement of the way *he* intended for things to happen. Scraps of Patti's conversation with Dan Davis insidiously crept into her mind. Which of the ex-cowboy's descriptions best fit the man seated across from her, candlelight gleaming on his fair hair? Someone more interested in getting than giving? A person who offered the flame of passion the old man said wouldn't last, but led to a hearth of fire? Or was Charles one whose chief aim would be to love and cherish her, and make her happy?

Patti wondered again when Charles took her home. Her escort's good-night kisses stirred her yet raised more questions. Curled up on her couch, she tried to pinpoint why she felt uneasy.

"It could be what Mr. Davis said," she admitted. "A burned child dreading the fire reaction. Maybe I'm just not ready to seri-

ously consider someone right now. Anyone."
She paused. "Lord, what if You've sent
Charles into my life for a purpose?" Patti
wrestled with her problem until her brain
grew too weary to concentrate. At last she
knelt, put herself, Charles, and the future
into God's hands, and went to bed.

An extremely busy day in Outpatient kept
Patti overtime the next day and made her
late in getting to the Transitional Care Unit.
Mr. Davis, bursting with impatience, barely
waited until she seated herself before saying, "Doc says I'm doin' so well, he has to
discharge me in a few days. I'm headin' for
home. Why don't you come with me?"

"You want me to go to Montana?" Patti
gasped.

"Sure. My log cabin's got two bedrooms.
I'm also old enough to have a nurse stayin'
with me for a spell without causin' talk."
His blue eyes twinkled and his laugh
rumbled out. "If I remember right, you said
you ain't had a vacation for some time. Kalispell in early summer's like a bit of heaven.
It has everything: mountains, lakes, valleys,
hiking, horseback riding, boat and raft trips.
Ever been to Glacier National Park? If you
stick around until the sawbones says okay,
I'll take you across the park on the Going-

31

to-the-Sun Highway." He cackled. "You'll think you are, going to the sun, that is. It's mighty high."

Patti thrilled to the idea. "It sounds wonderful," she wistfully said. "I haven't been to Glacier since I was a kid. We stayed at Fish Creek and Two Medicine, but didn't take the Going-to-the-Sun Highway. It spit snow the early June day we started across from the western side. We were on the outside of the road and Mom grew really nervous. Dad turned and went back."

"Good idea. If you're a mite shaky in high places, you do better to travel from east to west. That way, you're on the inside of the road almost the whole way." Dan Davis's eyes brightened. "Will you come? The folks who bought the Running H said I was welcome to come stay a spell with them any time." His strong forefinger traced a slanting *H* on the arm of his chair. "I'm certain they'd make us welcome and you could see what ranching is all about. Nothin' fancy or duded up about the Hoffs. Just plain, hardworkin' folk like Sarah and me."

A rush of blood to her head made Patti feel dizzy. "You really mean it?"

"Never meant anything more in my life." A callused hand rested on hers. "Sometimes gettin' away from ourselves helps sort things out," he observed.

Patti caught his meaning in a flash. What a God-given opportunity for her to gain a fresh perspective toward the hospital and her restlessness. Most of all, toward Charles's proclamation. A few days away, especially on a working cattle ranch, would surely restore her badly-shaken confidence in her ability to make decisions. She turned her palm upward and squeezed the hard fingers. "If I can get a leave of absence, I'll go," she promised. Patti released Mr. Davis's hand and jumped up.

"Don't go away." She laughed at her absurdity. "As if you would! I mean, I'll be right back." She knew she babbled and didn't care. Who wouldn't, with the dream of a lifetime coming true? Now if she could arrange for leave, everything would be perfect.

The first roadblock was her supervisor. Luckily, the older nurse had stayed to confer with the next swing shift's charge nurse. Patti held in her excitement until the nurse moved away, then exploded, "I have a chance to go home to Montana with Mr. Davis and spend time on a cattle ranch. Please, may I take vacation time?"

The astonished supervisor raised her eyebrows. "You mean it? Of course you may go! How much time do you want, or need?"

"Two weeks? Mr. Davis has some plans for after his recuperation."

"No problem." A wide smile creased the caring face. "So dreams really do come true. Go for it, Thompson. You'll come back rested and of more use than ever. Not that you aren't and haven't been a good nurse," she added. "It's just that you haven't had a real vacation for so long, it will be a real shot in the arm."

Two days later, family and friends informed of her impending departure for wild and still woolly (according to Mr. Davis) western Montana, Patti faced her last obstacle before leaving. Packed bags littered the blue rug of her suite. Security had been notified of her absence. Her fellow nurses had clamored for postcards and ribbed her about her elderly boyfriend.

"Too bad he doesn't have a good-looking son," April Andrews sighed when the twins dropped in to say good-bye.

"Grandson would be more appropriate," her twin sister Allison pointed out. "Mr. Davis is at least seventy years old, even though he doesn't look it." She roguishly cocked her brown head. "If you need help handling all the handsome Kalispell cowboys, don't hesitate to send for us!"

Patti blushed. Her color deepened when April volunteered, "What does your handsome pilot think about being deserted? Want me to look after him while you're gone? He's better looking than any cowboy."

"He's been out of town," Patti told the grinning nurse. "I left a message on his answering machine. Thanks, but no thanks, April, for your obviously self-sacrificing offer. Charles Bradley doesn't need a nanny."

Allison shouted with laughter at her sister's expense. "That's telling her! Come on, April. Our room looks like a hurricane hit it. Have a great time, Patti. You really deserve it."

Patti warmed to the genuine affection in the girl's face. "Thanks. See you when I get back." She closed the door that led into the corridor and their room.

Heavy pounding battered her outside door. "Who is it?" Patti called. Although security patrolled the hospital grounds, she knew better than to open the door that led to a parking lot without identifying her caller.

"Charles."

Patti flung it wide. "How nice! I didn't think I'd see you before —"

The young pilot strode into the room and furiously demanded, "What do you think you're doing?"

Patti had never seen him so upset. "Didn't you receive my message?"

"Of course I did," he shouted. Strong hands shot out and fastened on her slim shoulders. "Are you crazy, taking off with someone who could die at any minute? Why are you going to Kalispell, of all places? What am I supposed to do while you're gone, sit around and twiddle my thumbs?" The edge to his voice was jagged enough to cut steak.

Anger licked at Patti's veins. "You're hurting me." She wrenched free and rubbed her sore shoulders. "Why are you acting like this? It's my chance for an all-expense-paid vacation, one I couldn't have without Mr. Davis. I explained all that in the message I left on your answering machine."

Some of Charles's rage died. Patti saw his struggle to become the charming pilot who first attracted her.

"I'm sorry," he said heavily. "I never want to do anything to hurt you. The thought of coming home to Seattle without knowing you're here threw me off balance." He held out his arms and his face took on a pleading expression. "Forgive me, please, Patti. I hate the idea of anyone else doing things for you. I spend hours thinking of special places to take you and planning what we'll do after we're married. I love you so much."

The contrition in his voice touched Patti's tender heart. Yet a nagging feeling of something important she needed to remember kept her from responding the way she knew he expected.

"I think you'd better go, Charles," she told him.

"Are you still angry with me? I don't blame you if you are. I acted like a jerk." He took her hands and gently kissed each palm.

Patti withdrew her hands and stepped back. "I'm shocked and disappointed in you and need time to think. Good night, Charles. Good-bye, actually. I won't see you before we leave tomorrow."

"Try to think of me kindly," he begged. The misery in his eyes intensified. "I can't ask you to forget, but please forgive me. You're my whole world, Patti. Sun, moon, and stars." Strangely enough, the trite expression didn't sound ridiculous coming from him, as it would from other men. Charles bowed his head and walked toward the outside door.

She longed to reassure him, to erase the lost little boy look in his face. She couldn't. The haunting feeling that something vital lurked just beyond her recognition locked Patti's lips as firmly as she locked the door behind her no-longer-welcome guest. She sank to the couch, knowing she would never sleep unless she recalled whatever lay hidden.

It took Patti a long time. She replayed the ugly scene over and over in her mind without finding the trace of a clue. Nothing came until she switched her attention to Mr. Davis. Suddenly scattered phrases from her cowboy friend's little "sermon on marriage" knocked at the door of her mind and gained entrance. *A heap of so-called love . . . demandin' . . . self-seekin' . . . treats folks terrible . . . thinks sayin' 'I love you' will make everything right . . . a ragin' flame . . . a hearth of fire . . . burns out . . . becomes nothin' but ashes.*

Tonight a man she admired, even wondered if she could love, had exhibited all the traits Dan Davis decried. Charles Bradley had claimed his actions sprang from feelings so tremendous he couldn't stand the thought of being apart from her, or seeing others do things for her. Patti slowly shook her head. A few days earlier she had watched a small child in a store bellow to get his own way. Although Charles was close to thirty years old, he so dangerously resembled the child it made her shudder. *What might a man who left bruises on the woman he was trying to impress do to her, once he possessed her? What would marriage be with a man immature enough to fly into a rage over nothing?*

"I'm glad I'm going away," she whispered to her heavenly Father. "I'll have time to think. I truly need it. If Charles is really like I saw him tonight, I'll know You've prepared this way of escape."

Patti stood under the shower for a long time, allowing the warm water to sluice away some of her stress. She towel-dried her short hair and crawled into bed. In an amazingly short time, she fell asleep. Hours later she struggled back to consciousness, wide awake in the darkness of the room. A question hovered on her lips, and she said aloud, "Lord, when Charles grabbed me and began shouting, he asked why I was going to Kalispell, *of all places.* Why would he say something like that?"

The night offered no answers. Patti eventually fell asleep again. The next time she opened her eyes, a gorgeous early morning chased away the shadows, making her wonder if the unpleasant incident the night before had only been a bad dream. Fading footsteps outside her door that led to the parking lot set her pulse quick-stepping. She hurried into a robe and called, "Who is it?"

No one answered.

"Who's there?" she demanded.

The sound of a car motor starting hummed in her ears.

Heart beating furiously, Patti ran out her corridor door. She beat on April and Allison Andrews' door. "Quick. Let me in. It's Patti."

The thud of feet landing on the floor and a startled exclamation followed. Allison opened the door.

"Patti? What's wrong?" Sleep clouded her eyes.

She slid inside and raced toward a window with a view of the parking lot. She was too late. Nothing moved in the now-silent lot.

"Patti, what *is* it?" a fully awake Allison cried. April just stared.

The Outpatient nurse told them. "I have to call Security," she finished, starting back to her apartment.

Allison snatched her sleeve. "You aren't going back until someone checks it out," she insisted. April grabbed the phone and reported what had happened. Minutes later, a patrol car swung into the parking lot. A guard jumped out. Patti and the pajama-clad twins ran back to the other apartment.

She unlocked the outside door, opened it, and gasped.

A gigantic florist's bouquet overflowed the guard's outstretched arms.

Patti sagged against the door frame. "What on earth —"

The guard grinned broadly. "Looks like someone didn't think you'd be up, so he left a present. Any reason to suspect it isn't legitimate?"

"N–no." Patti's gaze riveted on a small envelope with her name scrawled across the front. She ripped it open and felt streaks of color stain her face.

"Well?" April, the more impatient of the twins, asked.

"It's a false alarm," Patti replied in a small voice. "A–a friend who had to leave town early dropped them off."

Allison glanced at the size of the bouquet the guard courteously carried in and set on a table.

"Some friend." She yawned and glanced at her watch. "Now that the excitement's over, I may as well shower."

Patti hid the card in the pocket of her robe. "Sorry I bothered everyone."

"Hey, that's what friends and security guards are for," the irrepressible April told her before she trailed after her sister.

41

"She's right, you know," the guard said seriously. "Better a false alarm than to ignore anything the least bit suspicious." He nodded. "Have a great vacation, Nurse Thompson." He walked back to the patrol car and drove off.

Patti stepped inside, locked her door, and reread the note.

I have an early flight. I hope this isn't too little, too late. Have a wonderful time, my darling, and try to forgive me. I'll be waiting.

All my love,
Charles

CHAPTER 3

When Patti appeared in the staff dining room clad in a denim jeans and jacket outfit with a red bandanna loosely circling her neck, loud sighs greeted her from her two best nurse friends. Red-haired Lindsey O'Shea wore the cotton dress she kept on hand and changed into after her night shift on Surgery. Tiny Japanese-American Shina Hyde's crisp rose-pink pants uniform showed she was ready to begin a day in Obstetrics.

"Wish I could show up this time of day dressed like a cowgirl," Lindsey complained. "Yippee-ki-oh-ki-ay. She's off into the wild blue yonder."

"Mixed metaphors," Patti retorted. "Don't be silly. The Air Force goes off into the wild blue yonder. *I'm* headin' for Big Sky country, pardner." Laughter spilled over like a waterfall. She touched the red rosebud pinned to her lapel. Taking Charles's preposterously large peace offering with her to Montana had been out of the question. Patti had filched the bud and donated the floral arrangement to the Information desk in the lobby.

"Get along, little dogie," tiny Shina sang out.

"I had a long little dogie once." Lindsey's warm brown eyes twinkled golden motes of mischief. "It came from Joe's hot dog stand and gave me indigestion."

"We certainly are jealous this morning," Patti told her friends sweetly. "I'll think of you slaving away here while I'm riding the range and chasing rustlers."

"Thanks a bunch, but didn't rustlers go out with Prohibition?" Lindsey hunched her shoulders and yawned without waiting for a reply. "I had a night to remember in Surgery. Actually, a night to forget. I could use a couple of weeks of R&R on a ranch — rest and recuperation to you uninformed nurses."

Shina's silky dark brows shot up. "We aren't uninformed. It's just been so long since Patti and I had any R&R we can't remember what it's like, let alone what it means."

"Right!" Lindsey stumbled to her feet. One hand dropped to Patti's shoulder.

"Have a great vacation. Mind your manners and don't fall off a horse."

"Yes, Mother," Patti meekly replied.

Shina's laugh trilled out. After a hasty glance at her watch, she also stood. "Sorry to eat and run, but duty calls." She smiled at Patti. "I hope your vacation is perfect."

"It will be. Absotively, posilutely." *Especially since Charles did all he could to make things right,* she silently added. She touched the rosebud again, blushing when her friends eyed it curiously but mercifully refrained from asking questions.

It didn't take long to finish breakfast and walk to the Transitional Care Unit. Patti checked with the nurse at the desk and learned all the necessary paperwork had been completed for discharging Mr. Davis. Nothing remained except to put him in a wheelchair.

"There you are." His weathered face brightened when Patti walked into his room. Polished cowboy boots that nevertheless showed signs of hard wear replaced slippers. A well-used Stetson lay in his lap. A key ring dangled from his fingers. His blue eyes twinkled when he held it out to her. "Ever herd a bronco?"

"Excuse me?" Enlightenment came. "Oh, you mean a Ford Bronco."

"Yep. I got mine just before they quit makin' them in '96. It's been corralled in the parking garage since I came here."

She couldn't help teasing him. "Was that 1996 or 1896 when you bought it?"

The old cowboy's laugh boomed loud in the quiet room. "I may be old, but I ain't that old, young lady. Are you packed and ready to go?" He hopped out of his chair like a long-legged grasshopper escaping an enemy.

"Whoa, there. I have to get a wheelchair," she protested.

He bristled. "Naw. I walked in here on my own legs. I'll go out the same."

"Sorry, it's a hospital rule."

Mr. Davis looked doubtful. "Well, all right, but I don't need mollycoddlin'. Doc says I'm better than new. Want me to do a little jig to prove it?"

Patti grinned at his high spirits. "Naw," she parroted. "Let's get out of here before they decide you're getting too big for your britches and keep you."

"You mean ridin' too high in the saddle, but it's all the same thing." He dropped into the wheelchair she brought, grinned at the staff who gathered to tell him good-bye, and heaved a sigh of relief when she wheeled him down the corridor. "There's a mighty

46

fine bunch of people here, but I can't wait to get outside and breathe some fresh air."

Patti silently echoed his wish. She left him close to an exit door and hurried to the parking garage. The prospect of two whole weeks spent mostly outdoors loomed brighter than the red Ford Bronco she drove out into the sunlight. Mr. Davis contentedly settled into the passenger seat, rolled down his window, and relaxed after asking, "Would you rather have the window shut? There's air conditioning."

"Not yet, at least. I like fresh air, too." Patti stopped in the lot by her apartment, tied the red bandanna gypsy fashion over her head, and ran in for her bags. It took only a short time to stow them away and thread city streets until they came to Interstate 90 and joined eastbound traffic.

"The prettiest way is through Stevens Pass," Mr. Davis told her. "But Snoqualmie is the fastest." Longing colored his voice and Patti quickly agreed they should go by way of Snoqualmie. Now he burst out, "Montana or bust!"

Patti had the feeling he wanted to bellow like one of the bulls on the Running H, but refrained to keep from distracting her while she drove. Sympathy rose like a high tide. How glad she was to be going with him!

"I'm curious. Why is the ranch called the Running H, when the Hoffs only bought it recently? Shouldn't it be the Running D, for Davis?"

He laughed with an exuberance that tilted the corners of her mouth upward. "It was the Running H when Sarah and I bought it. Names have a way of stickin' in those parts. We never even considered changin' it. Too much bother, with our critters wearing the H brand."

Patti impulsively said, "You'll never know how grateful I am, Mr. Davis."

"What for?" He looked genuinely surprised. "You're the one who took time for an old man." He shifted in his seat. "Since we're away from the hospital, how about callin' me Dan? Every time I hear Mr. Davis, I think folks are referrin' to my daddy, God rest his soul."

"I'll be glad to, if you will call me Patti. So far, you've either called me nurse, or young lady, or nothing at all," she reminded him.

"Patti it is," he told her heartily. "How do you like herdin' my bronc?"

"I love it. Living at the hospital, I haven't needed a car, although of course I have a license." She changed lanes, glorying in the open stretch of road before them. "It's been years since I went to eastern Washington. Everything's new to me. I can hardly wait to see what's over the next hill or around the bend."

"Patti Thompson, you're a thoroughbred," Dan told her. "You also ain't seen nothin' yet."

The capable nurse nodded. They soon swept over the pass and down the east side of the Cascade Mountain Range through impressive scenery. Timbered rolling hills gave way to sparsely treed slopes. The travelers stopped in Ellensburg for cool drinks, then headed northeast, still on I-90.

They reached Spokane in early afternoon, after traveling across desolate stretches that impressed neither of them. Patti found it hard to believe the barren desert only needed water to blossom until she saw the difference irrigation made.

With every mile, more color returned to the ex-rancher's lined face, more sparkle to his faded eyes. In Spokane, he directed Patti to a family restaurant not far from the freeway.

"Even beats the food at Shepherd of Love," he bragged.

The home-style meal more than lived up to his raves. At her host's urging, Patti finished with warm peach cobbler topped with whipped cream.

"I should have bought my jeans a size larger, if this is how we're going to eat," she groaned.

"I'm a pretty good hand at cookin' when I have to," Dan modestly told her. "Don't worry. You'll work it off at the Running H."

A few qualms attacked. "Are you sure the Hoffs will want to take in a stranger?" She fought down disappointment. "Don't worry if things don't work out. I'll still have a good vacation."

"No need to fret about the Hoffs. They never met a stranger. Besides, you ain't a stranger to me," he gruffly told her. "That's all that counts." He glanced at his watch. "Reckon it's about time to get goin'."

"We aren't driving clear to Kalispell today, are we?" A little frown creased Patti's forehead and darkened her eyes. "We've already come close to three hundred miles and are only about halfway there."

Dan shook his white head. "I've done it, but we ain't in that kind of hurry. Coeur d'Alene's a nice place, not far over the Idaho border. I know a good quiet motel. It has a swimmin' pool and a cafe next to it that serves the best flapjacks this side of the Running H."

"Coeur d'Alene sounds fine. Food doesn't

50

right now," Patti told him. When they were back on the road she mused, "It would be fun to know where some of the places we'll be got their names."

"Folklore says the word Idaho may have come from the Shoshone Indian words *Ee dah how!* It means 'The sun comes down the mountains,' or 'It is morning,' " Dan informed her. "Idaho is also called The Gem of the Mountains. Coeur d'Alene was founded as a fort in the 1890s by General Sherman, and named after the Indian tribe. Loosely translated from French, it means *hard-hearted.* Don't let sparklin' Lake Coeur d'Alene and the peaceful area around it you see now fool you. Winter can be as hard-hearted as a greedy landlord."

Patti laughed at his analogy and continued her lesson. "How about Montana?"

Dan's craggy face softened. "Spanish for 'mountainous.' Early travelers took a good long gander at the sun glistenin' on our snow-capped peaks and named it 'Land of Shining Mountains.' It's also called Big Sky country and the Treasure State. Kalispell's an Indian word meaning 'land going to the sun.' That's where they got the name for Glacier Park's Going-to-the-Sun Highway."

"You are an absolute gold mine of information!" she marveled.

The cowboy sage snorted. "A feller who doesn't take time to know about his town and state ain't fit to live there." He settled back and gazed out the window.

Patti concentrated on her driving, enjoying every minute of it. The more space she put between herself and Shepherd of Love, the lighter her spirits became.

Time enough to deal with uncertainties and Charles Bradley when she flew home.

"I am so glad you had the Bronco in Seattle," she said. "You see so much more driving than flying."

Dan didn't respond for such a long time Patti glanced over at him, wondering if he were asleep. She quickly returned her gaze to the road. Dan's faraway expression showed he wasn't ignoring her. Far more likely he had forgotten his nurse's presence. The dreaming light in his eyes betrayed him. Mind and heart had outrun the Bronco in reaching the land he loved, the land of shining mountains where he met and married Sarah McClelland so long ago.

Envy settled on Patti, light as butterfly wings. She did not begrudge Dan Davis his memories. She yearned for such a love to one day enter the gates of her heart. She trembled. Love was not always instant recognition, as with Dan and Sarah. Some love came quietly, stealing through the strongest barricades on kitten feet.

Hands steady on the wheel, a passage of Scripture came to mind. Patti remembered her mother reading it to her again and again, in a voice hushed with the same wonder that touched the small girl's listening ears.

And he said, Go forth, and stand upon the mount before the Lord. And, behold, the Lord passed by, and a great and strong wind rent the mountains, and brake in pieces the rocks before the Lord; but the Lord was not in the wind: and after the wind an earthquake; but the Lord was not in the earthquake: And after the earthquake a fire; but the Lord was not in the fire: and after the fire a still small voice. 1 Kings 19:11–12.

How would love come to her? In wind, earthquake, or fire? Or through a still, small voice assuring her all was well? Tears welled. Patti impatiently shook them away. God had granted one of her most treasured dreams by allowing her this interlude to draw closer to Him and provide time to listen for His still small voice. How ungrateful of her to cry for more, demanding that He also provide a mate!

Dan Davis's voice recalled her to the present.

"Take the next exit," he advised.

"All right." Patti closed the door to her thoughts, swung off the freeway and into Coeur d'Alene, a tranquil town that belied the meaning of its name. The motel Dan recommended hadn't changed. Its owners welcomed the ex-cowboy and his nurse as if they were long lost friends. Later in the evening, the travelers drove partway around Lake Coeur d'Alene. Patti drank in the resinous, pine-scented air, marveled at the sky's deep blueness reflected in the lapping water, and felt even more of the tension that had plagued her seep away. She awakened from a night of untroubled, uninterrupted sleep when her stomach rumbled.

"Lead me to those flapjacks," she told Dan in the motel lobby. Patti's professional eye noted how rested he appeared, and the renewed sparkle in his faded blue eyes.

After an enormous breakfast, they headed the Bronco into the rising sun and began the mountainous drive across Idaho and through the Bitterroot Range to Missoula.

"Do you mind if I sing?" Patti asked. "I'm so bursting over with all this beauty, it's hard to hold it inside."

"Go ahead," Dan told her. "I'll grumble along." He did, adding a surprisingly mellow bass accompaniment to Patti's rendition of "This Is My Father's World."

The Bronco ran smoothly, eating up the miles as if they were inches. Patti couldn't remember enjoying a drive more.

They lunched in Missoula at another of Dan Davis's favorite haunts, although Patti had sworn after breakfast she couldn't eat another morsel until dinner. She simply wasn't able to resist the cafe's homemade vegetable soup. Or the cornbread that melted in her mouth. Before she climbed back in the Bronco to head north on U.S. 93, she loosened the leather belt around her trim waist and warned, "You'd better get me exercising soon or my clothes won't fit."

The white-haired ex-cowboy fastened his seat belt and turned so he faced her squarely.

"I did some thinkin' about that last night. What say we hang around Kalispell a few days, then head east? We'll follow the Middle Fork of the Flathead River from West to East Glacier and stay there or at Browning. Some folks make the circle in one day, but we want time for stoppin' and lookin'."

His eyes twinkled. "Goin' that way also

fixes it so we come from east to west and hug the cliff side on most of the Going-to-the-Sun Highway, also called Going-to-the-Sun Road. Logan Pass is over 6600 feet. Lake McDonald's also well worth seein'. Once I saw that stretch of country, I never had a hankerin' to visit the Swiss Alps." He laughed sheepishly. "Sound like a tour guide, don't I? Anyway, you'll like it."

"Good," Patti enthusiastically replied. "I've liked almost everything so far."

White eyebrows raised in amusement. "Like I said before, you ain't seen nothin' yet. There's the National Bison Range a short piece up the road. We'll stop a spell, if you like. Flathead Lake's after that, then home."

The yearning in his voice made Patti blink. "A log cabin."

"Yes. And the Running H. I know it ain't mine, but it doesn't matter. The ranch will always be home to this stove-up, tired old cowpoke."

Patti's face must have shown signs of argument for Dan chuckled.

"Not so bad for an old-timer, actually." She felt his keen gaze rake her face. "I figure stayin' at the ranch will be the best part of your vacation, so we'll save it for last." He chuckled again. "If it was folks other than the Hoffs, I'd say go first, so they wouldn't fuss. Ma Hoff ain't that kind. Her floors are clean enough to eat from all the time and she won't start repaperin' just 'cause we're comin'. She'll throw a couple more beans in the pot, be glad if you help peel potatoes, and set us places at the table."

"I'm glad," Patti exclaimed. "I know you said we'd be welcome, but so many people feel they need to jump in and practically remodel if they know someone's coming! Knowing the Hoffs won't do that makes everything perfect." She broke off and squealed with excitement. "There's a buffalo!" She slowed to get a better view of the shaggy-shouldered beast that peered at the Bronco from beneath wicked-looking horns, then switched its tail and went on grazing.

"There are more. Look! There are some babies." Patti pulled to the side of the road and gazed entranced. Seeing buffaloes in their native habitat was a far cry from viewing the species in a zoo. "That's funny. The little ones are yellowish-red, instead of brownish-black like the others."

"Calves always are," Dan explained. "Bison, that's the proper handle for these critters in the U.S. and Canada, have their young in May or June. Once in awhile, a bison lives as much as thirty to forty years.

The bull that leads the herd watches out for the mother cows. He helps protect the calves from enemies."

"Better than some fathers," Patti mumbled. She found it hard to tear her fascinated gaze from the herd, but at last drove on. Many miles still lay between them and Kalispell, the "land going to the sun."

"Is your log cabin like the ones we've seen so far?" she asked a little later. "They're so homey looking."

"A mite bigger."

Patti wondered at the terse answer but decided the prospect of getting home was flooding Dan with memories. She searched her mind for a subject to get him talking and decided against it. Such a ploy would be an intrusion. A cardinal rule of nursing was to respect patients' privacy.

One instructor had drilled into Patti's class, "Never forget what Ecclesiastes 3 says: 'To every thing there is a season, and a time to every purpose under the heaven.' Add this to the list: 'a time to speak and a time to be still.' Simply being there for another human being is often the most effective way to aid healing. Words too often fail. Compassion flowing from your hearts never will."

How wise the teacher had been! Dozens of times Patti had heeded the advice burned into her soul as much by the look in her beloved mentor's face as the words themselves. A lightning glance toward Dan Davis disclosed his absorption in his own world. All he needed from her was to be driven home as safely and rapidly as her capabilities and Montana state law allowed.

Dan didn't speak again until they reached Kalispell. Then he turned shining eyes toward her and gave directions. Patti felt his curbed impatience. She recognized part of him wanted to leap forward like a mountain lion toward its prey. The vision of the cowboy he had been, hurrying himself and his tired horse home toward home and lighted windows, misted her eyes. *Thank You, Lord, for allowing me to be with Dan,* she silently prayed. *I'm glad this homecoming isn't at night. I couldn't bear having him return to a dark cabin.*

A few minutes later, Patti pulled into a gravel drive and realized how beautifully God had answered her prayer. *Dark cabin? Anything but!* Late afternoon sunlight mellowed the logs of Dan Davis's home. It turned each sparkling window to molten gold. Long and far larger than she had expected, the "cabin" nestled close to the ground like an infant cuddled against her mother's breast. A host of cottonwoods swayed in a slight breeze that cooled Patti's warm forehead. They dipped and fluttered their leaves, bowing before the guest.

Dan silently unlocked and opened the large front door circled by wild roses broadcasting their pink perfume.

"Welcome home, my dear," he said huskily.

Touched by his courtliness, Patti stepped across the threshold, into a room so soul-satisfying it eclipsed all her vague hopes and expectations.

CHAPTER 4

The inside of Dan Davis's log cabin home blazed with color, yet retained quietude and a sense of peace. Patti Thompson crooned with delight when she stepped into the living room. Deep green, plushy carpet made her feel she trod a forest floor. A few brightly woven Indian blankets hung like tapestries on the off-white walls. Sunlight shining through many windows laid a golden patina over the room. An enormous multicolored rock fireplace served as the focal point for the main room, which stretched at least twenty feet.

The portrait of a laughing girl in a fluffy white dress and hairstyle of the early forties hung above the fireplace mantel. Patti's first glance into the dark eyes gave her the curious sensation Sarah McClelland Davis quite approved her coming. It provided the final touch to make the upcoming vacation perfect.

Dan walked toward a door at the right side of the generous room. "Here's your home away from home, as they say. I'm on the opposite side. Both bedrooms have their own bathrooms. Kitchen and dinin' room are at the back." He threw wide the door. "How about we do some washin' up, then go out fer supper and do our grocery shoppin' on the way back?" His eyes twinkled. "Like I said, I'm quite a hand at cookin'."

"Sounds good to me." Patti walked through the open door and stopped short. Her first glimpse of her new abode made her wonder if she had died and gone to heaven. The charming bedroom faced west, as did the living room. The sun was putting on its best imitation of King Midas, painting the walls with gold overlay. A polished cross-section of pine with the motto "I will lift up mine eyes unto the hills, from whence cometh my help" burned into the wood hung on the wall. Patti dropped to her knees by the brightly blanketed bed, too filled with peace and gratitude for words, yet knowing God would understand. In the short time before she rose and did a lightning wash-up job, the western sky — and the off-white walls of her room — had changed to violet and strawberry pink.

"How do you like my shack?" Dan eagerly

asked when she stepped back into the living room.

"Shack? More like a log mini-mansion! I could be happy here for the rest of my life, with —" She paused and felt a rich blush mount from her neck.

"With the right man," her host finished. "Of course, you wouldn't want to give up your nursin', but that could be arranged." After they got back in the Bronco, he asked, "How would you feel about leavin' Shepherd of Love?"

Patti kept her gaze on the road ahead. "I never even considered working anywhere else until lately." She told him how restless she had grown with her friends married, touched lightly on her bad experience with Bart Keppler. "I started to talk it over with the hospital director one day, then decided I was not ready," she confessed. "Your invitation was a God-send, in capitals. I knew I needed to get away, but not how much until we actually started."

"I thought you might. We take the next left," he directed. Nothing more was said about Patti's career for some time. The proprietors of the small but spotless restaurant greeted Dan as if he'd been gone a century and warmly welcomed Patti. After a delicious meal and a productive trip to a nearby supermarket, the ex-cowboy and nurse headed back to the log cabin in the cottonwoods.

Apprehension touched Patti when she turned into the gravel driveway. Light poured through the living room windows.

"That's funny. I don't remember you switching on a light," she told her companion.

"I didn't." He opened his door and smiled at her in the dim glow from the dome light. "I got me one of those newfangled devices that turns lights off and on at dawn and dusk. It's a lot better."

Better than coming home to a dark house and no Sarah, Patti thought. To cover the emotion welling up within her, she sprang out of the Bronco and began filling her arms with grocery sacks.

Dan immediately complained, "You modern gals make it downright hard for a feller to be a gentleman." He reached for a bulging bag.

"Oh, no, you don't," she said. "I do the heavy lifting around here for awhile."

He snorted. "Just what I expected. We ain't been here half a day and already you're gettin' mighty bossy." He took the sting out of his words by adding, "Just like my Sarah when she caught me doin' something I shouldn't."

"That's the nicest compliment you could give me," Patti called after him when he went ahead to unlock and open the front door.

Dan stopped and grinned. The light from the room silvered his hair to a halo.

"I reckon it is."

It didn't take long to stow their booty. Capacious knotty pine cupboards in both the pine-paneled kitchen and adjoining dining room added to the attractiveness of the rooms, as did ruffled white curtains at the windows.

"Everything's so clean," Patti tactlessly marveled.

Her host bristled. "I have never lived in a pigsty and I don't aim to start now."

She felt terrible. "I'm sorry. It just surprised me to find it spotless when you've been gone some time."

Dan relaxed. "I normally do my own cleanin'." He hesitated and looked sheepish. "When I'm away, a neighbor comes in and gives it a once-over just before I'm due home." He complacently looked around the rooms. "Livin' alone means there ain't that much housework. Now, let's settle down and talk."

"Isn't that what we have been doing?"

Patti pertly asked.

Dan chuckled, strode back to the living room, and waited until she seated herself in a comfortable chair before dropping into its twin.

"I have a question for you. Is there something you've always wanted to do outside of nursin'?"

"You mean besides stay on a working cattle ranch for a time?" She curled deeper in the chair that held her like strong arms.

"A secret dream, maybe. One you never thought could come true."

Patti hesitated. She did have a dream, something she hadn't shared even with her best friends at Shepherd of Love. They knew nothing of the desire that periodically wakened, only to sigh and slumber again. Could she share her wish? Why not? Dan Davis had such insignificant contact with her normal world, her secret would be safe with him.

Patti laced her fingers together. Her voice sounded small in her own ears. "I've always wondered if I could draw or paint."

"Did you ever try?"

"I dabbled when I was a kid, but have been too busy since," she told him.

"Too much else to do. I studied hard in high school and college. Then came nursing training. Ever since, my job has kept me busy."

"Is lack of time the only reason?"

She gazed at him wide-eyed. "Are you trying to psychoanalyze me?"

Dan shook his head. "Naw. It's just that years of livin' sometimes help me see things in folks." She didn't reply and he added, "Most folks find time for what they really want to do, unless they're a wee bit afraid to try."

Patti felt as if he had sent an arrow bull's-eye into her vulnerable heart.

"You mean because I — people think they'll fail? Isn't that a good enough reason?"

"I reckon folks like Thomas Edison and that Alexander Graham Bell feller would disagree. They tried and failed a heap of times before succeedin'. Good thing they did. Otherwise, we'd be sittin' in the dark without telephones."

Patti digested what he said then glanced up from the fingers she had been intently observing and into sympathetic blue eyes. "I've always been a perfectionist," she explained. "I want to do things well, or not at all. Maybe I've used being busy as an excuse."

"The good Lord don't expect us to always

be the best," Dan reminded her. "I didn't stay long on a buckin' bronc the first time I rode one! I up and climbed back on, though." He laughed, a delightful sound in the quiet room. "Some feller, I don't know who, hit the nail square on the head when he wrote:

Never a horse what couldn't be rode.
Never a cowpoke what couldn't be throwed.

"If you want to draw and paint, you owe it to yourself to try. You might find out it's a hidden talent. One that needs diggin' out and polishin' like a gold nugget." He grinned at her. "Remember Jesus tellin' about the slothful servant who brought down a good scoldin' on himself for hidin' his talent in the ground? I always felt it was a cryin' shame the galoot didn't have gumption enough to take his talent and make it grow."

Patti threw her hands into the air in mock surrender. "Will tomorrow be soon enough for me to purchase a sketch pad?" she meekly inquired. A mighty yawn followed. "Sorry. I don't think I could keep my eyes open enough tonight to draw anything more than my bath!"

The grumbling laugh Patti loved started at Dan's toes, worked up volume, and came out as a bellow. When he sobered, he suggested they read a Scripture and hit the sack. She nodded. Worn but agile fingers leafed through an equally worn Bible until they came to the parable of the talents. Patti couldn't remember ever taking it so personally. Heart thumping with determination, she privately vowed to use part of her vacation in finding out whether she had any artistic talent.

The next few days flew with the speed of light. Dan was fortunate in getting overnight reservations at East Glacier after someone canceled. If Patti lived to be older than the Rocky Mountains, she would never forget her trip across Glacier National Park. Words like spectacular, awe-inspiring, and sublime paled before reality. Coming home on the Going-to-the-Sun Road surpassed Patti's wildest expectations: jagged cliffs on her right; a rugged, seemingly bottomless canyon on her left. Although she'd never been squeamish about heights, she gave silent and fervent thanks they were on the inside most of the time.

Patti's newly awakened desire to draw increased. Dan graciously suggested they stop several times along the way.

"I'm content to lean against a pine tree and rusticate," he whimsically told her. "Take all the time you need. Walk. Drink it all in. Sketch, if you like. I'll be fine."

She couldn't resist giving him a big hug. In the relatively short time she'd known him, Patti had learned to love the former cowboy. He taught her untrained eyes to appreciate God's creation more than ever. The first time she laughed at an ungainly moose, Dan wryly reflected, "Either God sees beauty we're missin' or has a mighty good sense of humor most folks don't recognize!"

Patti reveled in every moment of the trip. "It's like my whole soul is expanding to match this vast country, God," she murmured, trying to capture a breathtaking view with inept strokes of a pencil. She scowled in exasperation.

The panorama before her needed far more skill than she possessed to capture it.

"When I get back to Seattle, I'm going to take an art class," she told Dan.

"Good idea," he heartily approved. "May I see your latest effort?"

She reluctantly handed it over. "This is how a mother must feel when she shows her baby to the world for the first time," she ruefully said.

Dan glanced from the sketch to the scene before them. "Not bad, Patti." He pointed to the pictured hint of peaks and a leafy branch thrust into the sky, then their living counterparts. "Your first impressions are bold, a lot better than where you've retouched. They show you have a keen eye and a grasp for what's there. Trainin' can help you learn how to make the most of your natural talent and add all the other stuff you need." He frowned. "I ain't an expert, but it seems you'd do better with color. Black and white's a mite stark."

Patti blushed with pleasure at his praise and quickly agreed. "I'll buy watercolors, or at least colored pencils, when I get back to Kalispell." She sighed and gathered up her paraphernalia. "I suppose we'd best go."

"We could stay longer, but it'd mean cuttin' into your time on the Running H," her white-haired companion teased. His brown face crinkled.

"No way!" Patti promptly contradicted. "This may be my only chance to stay on a ranch. I can't give it up. Even for all this." She waved around her.

Dan took a long time to answer. When he cleared his throat and spoke, Patti felt her friend chose each word carefully. "The room in my home's yours as long as you

71

want it. No charge for room and board. If you consider stayin' on for a time, we'll come back to Glacier. I can also take you a heap of other places."

Patti felt like a wishbone. The new and free part of her she'd discovered since coming to Montana longed to cut ties and accept. The other part clung to the security of Seattle and the hospital. How much did Charles Bradley have to do with her feelings? Patti shook her head. Right now, the handsome pilot seemed faraway, unreal. How would she feel when she saw him again?

Perhaps she only had a severe case of vacation madness, the affliction that often attacked travelers to different areas of the country. It sometimes led them into unwise, spur-of-the-moment decisions concerning relocation and career changes.

"I really appreciate the offer," she told Dan. "It's tempting, but it's also a long way from Seattle to Kalispell, and not just in miles."

"I know. I probably just have an old man's fancy. Don't fret about it. But remember, Patti, the door's wide open if you ever want to come."

"I will," she choked out. Tears spilled and an errant thought came. A short time ago she had told God she needed to be more independent and learn to make decisions without leaning on her friends, especially Lindsey and Shina. God certainly hadn't wasted any time putting her to the test.

The same thought recurred to Patti when she and Dan Davis took up residence at the Running H. They swiftly became part of the Hoff household. Ma and Pa, as they insisted on being called, stood on no ceremony with their guests.

"Dan says you want to be treated like one of the family," Ma announced. "Fine with Pa and me. We can always use more hands."

Patti thrilled to being considered a "hand" on the large ranch. Dan's grin showed his happiness at being back on the spread. Slouched in the saddle as if he were part of it, he spent hours teaching Patti to ride and filling her head with cowboy lore. He audibly regretted he wouldn't have time "on this trip" to teach her to shoot and rope.

She exchanged the mental fatigue that had disturbed her sleep in Seattle for physical weariness. It inevitably claimed her in sleep halfway through her nightly prayers. Resenting time away from the fascinating work of running a large ranch, Patti settled for a one-letter-will-have-to-do-for-all to her

nurse friends. In it, she ecstatically announced,

I can't remember being this rested in
ages. I recommend time on a ranch like
the Running H to anyone who needs
rejuvenating. We're up shortly after daylight, but that's okay, because we head for
bed a little after dark. I'm eating so much I
feel ashamed, yet ask for more. Ma Hoff
says I'm the best kitchen "flunky" she's
ever had and I enjoy every minute of it!

I won't go into all the other stuff I do, but
the Patti I've become since arriving in
Montana is a far cry from the poor thing
Bart Keppler deceived. I'd like to see him
try it now! Even if he fooled me (and I don't
think he could) nothing gets past Dan Davis. A cowhand from a neighboring ranch
looked me over a little too boldly to suit
Dan when we met on the range. Dan told
the guy if he had to gawk, he should go
stare in a store window.

My heart leaped to my throat. I could just
see the rowdy climbing down from his
horse and pounding my protector. He did
nothing of the sort. He took one look at
Dan's stony face and steely eyes,
mumbled an apology, and rode away (in
the words of my white-haired hero) "like a

whipped puppy."

Patti yawned. The pressing need to let her friends know she still remained in the land of the living couldn't keep her awake. She hastily scrawled her name and shoved the letter into a stamped, addressed envelope.

"I'm not satisfied, but there is far too much to tell in a letter," she justified herself.

Although sleepy, Patti had trouble falling asleep for the first time since coming to Montana. She replayed the events of the past twenty-four hours. She could recall nothing unusual. A glorious sunrise. The discovery time in the saddle had changed from stubborn endurance to actual enjoyment. Marveling at the vast numbers of cattle, each branded with the familiar *H*. Riding home in a kaleidoscope of color no one but the Master Artist could ever achieve. The western sky reflected every shade of red, orange, and yellow, then subtly turned to amethyst and deep purple against the clear blue.

Wait. There had been something a little different today. She and Dan had reined in their horses on a mesa miles away from the ranch buildings. Patti felt the view stretched forever. Dan warned they needed to start back soon. Before she could touch heels to her horse, a noise in the sky drew Patti's gaze up. A helicopter flew over them and headed northwest. The pilot waved. Patti waved back and asked, "Why is a helicopter out here?"

Dan shaded his eyes against the sun. "That's Mike Parker's Rescue Service chopper. I can't tell whether he's pilotin' it."

"Rescue chopper?" Patti visually followed the path of the helicopter. It looked like nothing more on earth than a giant, awkward white grasshopper trimmed with red markings and a bright red cross.

"Patti, my dear, we have people livin' in out-of-the-way places where medical help ain't to be had just for the askin'. We also have folks with less sense than God gave a goose visit this area." Dan warmed to his subject. "They come out here from who knows where, determined to rough it. More than likely, they end up in hot water. Or snow and ice. Or at the bottom of a hill they shouldn't have been climbin' in the first place. Mike Parker sends out medical help. His pilots know first aid and a whole lot more. They take a nurse with them and do everything from transporting seriously injured folks back here to deliverin' babies on the spot. I know of at least three little guys named Michael in honor of Parker."

Dan's eyes gleamed. "If you were livin' here, there's always a chance Mike could use you. How would you like bein' a flyin' rescue nurse?"

"I don't know. I haven't delivered any babies lately," she teased.

Now the thought of the odd conversation haunted Patti. *This Mike Parker must be a pretty special guy, one who really wanted to help others.* Her last waking thought was a pang of regret she wouldn't be around to meet him and the question, *Not that I'm going to stay, but I wonder what Mike Parker is like?* She fell asleep and dreamed a handsome pilot waved to her, then crawled inside a white helicopter marked in red and bearing a bright red cross. She watched with racing heart until pilot and helicopter became a mere speck against a flaming Big Sky sunset.

Morning did not lessen her curiosity concerning Mike Parker. At breakfast she said, "We saw a Rescue Service helicopter yesterday. What's the owner like?"

"Mike Parker?" Ma Hoff deftly slid a plate of hot biscuits onto the table.

"About fifty, balding, a little on the paunchy side. You couldn't ask for nicer people or better Christians than Mike and his wife. I don't know what folks around here would do without the flying hospital. It's saved a peck of lives."

"The helicopter isn't really a hospital," Pa Hoff corrected. He helped himself to a biscuit. "More like a flying first aid station."

Patti smothered her mirth in her napkin. Leave it to her to have romantic dreams about a middle-aged, married Rescue Service owner! Her smile died. Good grief! Was she so desperate to find someone with whom to share her life that she viewed every man she saw or heard about as a candidate for the position?

CHAPTER 5

Dan Davis took Patti Thompson through Glacier National Park the first weekend after they reached Kalispell. The following Sunday, which would be her last in Montana, they climbed into the Running H station wagon with the Hoffs and drove to church in Kalispell. The plain but well-filled chapel glowed with morning sunlight and rang with enthusiastic singing. Patti's heart overflowed. There was no stuffy, formal religion here, only the gospel, alive and real.

The minister looked nothing like mahogany-haired Terence O'Shea who tended the spiritual needs at Shepherd of Love, yet a common spirit reminded Patti of the hospital chaplain. After some contemplation she decided it was the unmistakable fact both believed every word they preached from the depths of their souls.

The Kalispell pastor had chosen the theme "Leave all and follow."

Patti drank in every word. She hated for the sermon to end, although the entire congregation crowded around to meet and welcome her.

"I want you to know Mike Parker," Dan Davis said. "Mike, this is Nurse Patti Thompson. I'm tryin' to rope her into stayin' in Kalispell."

About fifty. Balding. Paunchy. Ma Hoff's description brought a smile to Patti's lips when Mike's huge hand engulfed hers.

"We can always use more nurses in this part of the country," he said in a surprisingly gentle voice. "Right, Scott?" he asked someone just behind Patti.

"Right."

She turned toward the amused voice and was struck by the stillness of the tall man's face. Her first impression was that he was in his early thirties, rugged, and dependable, a man to be trusted. Short black hair topped a lean, tanned face. Finely chiseled lips wore a small smile that didn't reach his brown eyes, so dark they looked black.

"Miss Thompson, meet Stone Face Sloan, senior pilot for my Rescue Service."

"Scott," the tall man corrected.

Stone Face is more appropriate, Patti thought. *I'll bet you are solid granite when you believe you're right.* She held out her hand.

Surprise chased some of the impassiveness from the pilot's face. "You have a strong grip."

Patti sighed. "At least you didn't add 'for a woman.' I get that all the time."

A slight smile hovered on his lips. "I'll bet you do."

"I never could stand dead fish handshakes," she impulsively told him.

The clear, ringing laugh turned faces in their direction and made a world of difference in Scott Sloan's face. It reminded Patti of the way spring green softened bare branches after a long winter.

"Are you serious about relocating to Kalispell?" Scott asked.

Patti couldn't tell whether his polite question expressed interest or merely served to fill the silence. She also didn't know how to answer.

Dan Davis came to her rescue. "I'm serious. She's thinkin' about it. At least, I hope she is." He grinned at Patti.

A somber expression dulled Scott's eyes. "It's a good place to live. Nice meeting you, Nurse Thompson." He nodded to Mike and Dan, turned on his heel, and walked down the aisle, spine rigid and head held high.

The abrupt departure left Patti staring after him. Few young men walked away from Patti Thompson.

"Did I say something wrong?" she asked Mike Parker.

"Naw. Stone Face is like that sometimes. A real private person, if you know what I mean. He's also an ace pilot, best of my crew. I'd never have been able to sign him on if it hadn't been —"

"Sorry, Mike, but we have an appointment and it's getting late," a soft voice reminded. Its plump, gray-haired owner smiled at Patti. "This husband of mine tends to be forgetful now and then. I'm so glad you could come, Dear." She hurried Mike away.

Patti experienced disappointment totally out of proportion to the situation. Of all the times to be interrupted, just when the conversation became interesting. Reason tapped at her shoulder. Why should she care why the ace pilot whose nickname Stone Face fit perfectly flew for Parker's Rescue Service? She'd be gone in a few days and never see the man again.

The thought brought a feeling Patti couldn't identify. Dismay filled her, even while she told herself not to be an idiot. Scott Sloan was nothing to her but a courteous stranger who admired her grip.

Patti's mental scolding didn't help a bit. She couldn't help comparing her present feelings with the little crushes she used to have at church camp. The excitement of meeting new boys who sometimes drifted in from other states had always held a note of sadness. Knowing she'd never see them again once camp ended brought bittersweet twinges that kept new friendships from being perfect.

Strange she should feel the same way about the sober-faced pilot. She thought she'd outgrown such childish behavior. *Probably my vanity,* she decided. Scott Sloan had been polite but not interested. Perhaps he had a wife. Patti tried to dismiss him from her thoughts, but her ears pricked up like a bird dog's on the trail when the Hoffs talked about Scott on the way home.

"Anyone know why they call him Stone Face?" The question sounded casual, but Patti held her breath waiting for the answer.

"Folks privately speculate. No one knows for sure unless it's Mike Parker," Dan said. "It's obvious the boy's had a bad experience at one time or another, but that's his business."

Although Patti knew her friend didn't refer to her, she felt like a kindergartner corrected and sent to a corner in shame. She hid her reaction by saying, "It's hard to believe in a few days I'll be back on duty in Outpatient. I wonder if all this will seem as dreamlike and other-worldlike as Seattle seems now."

"You can always come back." Dan's hasty laugh couldn't quite camouflage the pathos in his simple statement. His blue eyes gleamed. "Only thing is, you might have to stay in the log cabin alone."

An alarm bell rang in her brain. "Is there something you're not telling me?"

"Just that the Hoffs have gotten used to having a cantankerous old ex-cowboy around the Running H this last week. They want me to move back out here." A quiver in his voice betrayed how much the suggestion thrilled him.

Relief rolled through Patti. "That's wonderful! You're coming, aren't you?"

"I reckon I'll take them up on it," Dan drawled.

"Once a cowpoke, always a cowpoke," Pa Hoff put in. He chuckled. "It will be good to have Dan here, especially when winter comes. Ma'd rather crochet and watch TV than play checkers, so I don't have anyone to beat since the kids married and left home."

Dan's white head snapped up. "You ol'

tumbleweed, you still ain't goin' to have anyone to beat."

"If I'm an ole tumbleweed, what's that make you?" Pa retorted. "You're older than I am by a long shot."

"That's just what my birth certificate says. Inside where it counts, I'm young and frisky as a colt," Dan loftily informed his soon-to-be checker rival. They wrangled all the way home, to Patti's amusement and delight.

The final few days rushed past like a herd of stampeding cattle. Patti found herself marking off what she called "lasts": the last batch of bread she helped Ma Hoff bake; the last time she tried to capture distant mountains with crayon and watercolors; the last ride to the mesa overlooking the peaceful valley. She came to the point where if Dan again asked her to stay, she knew she would weaken. How could she leave this busy, satisfying life? On the other hand, Shepherd of Love and countless patients needed her skills and training. Dan said no more. She knew his creed made it impossible to coerce. He had given the invitation. Now he would respect Patti's right to choose.

The day before Patti flew home, the Hoffs moved Dan to the ranch. Patti knew she would never forget the look in his eyes as long as she lived; a look of coming home to the Running H, where he belonged. Even the now-empty log cabin in Kalispell hadn't been able to replace the ranch in Dan's life.

Pa Hoff bluntly said, "You're welcome to stay with us, or you can have a cabin." He indicated one of several small log houses scattered a short distance from the ranch house. "You'll eat with us, of course."

Dan chose the cabin. Surrounded by memories and the opportunity for solitude when he needed it, he would also have the comfort of knowing friends who loved him were close by.

Patti clung to her cowboy friend when it came time to board the westbound plane. "I–I feel like I'm leaving part of me," she choked out. "It's been perfect."

His gnarled hand stroked her bright hair. "Steady, there. You'll be back."

The prophetic ring in his voice stiffened her backbone and she brushed the mist from her eyes. "I hope so."

A curious glint accompanied his, "You will. Mark my words. Now, get to gettin', young lady, or you'll be missin' that plane." Her last sight of Dan Davis was his standing ramrod straight, right hand flung high in a wave Patti felt was more a benediction than a farewell.

Montana receded behind the speeding plane. So did Idaho. Washington State appeared. By the time the plane touched down at SeaTac International Airport, Patti felt she had passed from one life to another.

"I wonder if going from earth to heaven is like this," she whispered. "Simply leaving one place and arriving at another and better one." Her analogy fell apart. At this point, she seriously questioned whether Seattle was the better place for her.

The question continued for a few days, then lost itself in a maze of work and Charles Bradley. After his noncommittal acceptance of her stay in Montana on their first date, he seemed singularly disinterested except concerning whom she had met in Kalispell.

"Dan Davis. The Hoffs and their hands. Mike Parker," Patti reported.

"Is that Parker's Rescue Service? Helicopter outfit?"

Her eyes opened wide. "You know him?"

Charles grunted. "I know of him. Started on a shoestring and has built up a pretty good business. Anyone else?"

She thought of Scott Sloan, but wrote him off as insignificant. Charles wouldn't care about a pilot who seldom smiled and excused himself as soon as possible after meeting the nurse Charles considered his. Neither did she mention the loutish rider Dan Davis had so effectively put in his place. Why risk an unpleasant show of temper?

You aren't being fair, a little voice inside chastised. *Charles is obviously doing everything he can to erase the memory of his temper fit.*

The young pilot continued on his best behavior. Patti gradually spent more and more time with him. She felt herself responding to his magnetic personality and genuine affection more intensely with every date.

"I think I'm falling in love," she announced to her shining-eyed reflection in the bathroom mirror late one evening after Charles brought her home. Yet unlike the times she had formerly shared with Lindsey and Shina, she hugged the new-found feelings close to her heart and bided her time. Love for a lifetime had to be more than thrilling to a man's nearness, listening for the ring of the phone. Even though Charles continued to plan for after they were married, Patti hesitated. "Why?" she asked her image. "He attends chapel with me as often as his flight schedule permits. My slightest wish really is his command, as the old cliché says. What more can I want?" The mirrored eyes darkened. The vivid lips drooped. Impatient with herself for allowing introspection to dim the memory of an exciting evening, she turned away and prepared for bed.

Dan Davis sent infrequent postcards. Ma Hoff supplemented them with brief scrawls that said everyone was well and happy and their new cowhand got younger every day. If Patti didn't believe it, Ma Hoff wrote, she should come see for herself, maybe spend Christmas at the ranch.

Patti's heart thumped. If things continued as smoothly as they were going now, she might be wearing a diamond long before Christmas. Charles made her feel so special, so loved, cherished, and protected.

"I wonder if the Hoffs and Dan would welcome a fiancé as warmly as they did me?" she pondered. The thought raised a blush Patti knew outshone a fiery Montana sunset, but when she answered the invitation, she only said her plans for Christmas were uncertain.

Summer in Seattle changed overnight to a herald of things ahead. Afternoon temperatures rarely reached eighty degrees. Nights ranged from forty-five to fifty degrees. One morning a hint of frost sparkled on the hospital lawn. Flowers still bloomed brightly, but here and there a branch showed brown or red. Patti took out her sadly neglected art materials and tried to recapture the log home in Kalispell. Instead of green, she chose a sunny yellow for the cottonwood leaves to see if she could create an autumn version of the scene that was never far from her mind.

The results stirred a slumbering desire. Regret flicked her conscience. Why hadn't she carried through with her plan to take lessons in drawing or painting? One word: Charles. He wanted her to be available when he flew in. Patti's lips curved upwards. Were people now really so different from earlier generations? For years, Dan Davis eagerly rode home to lighted windows and the woman who waited for him. Now Charles Bradley no less eagerly flew back to Seattle — and Patti — from wherever his flight orders carried him.

Patti felt a kinship with Sarah McClelland. Had her pulse quickened to the beat of hooves, the way Patti's did to Charles's quick knock at her door? Patti wondered. Did she fling wide the door to heart and house, as a certain nurse was learning to do? Did she stretch her arms out in welcome to the man she adored? Had Sarah experienced the same feeling all was well now that her man was home that meant so much to Patti?

Why wait longer to admit my love for Charles? Patti decided that when he came that night, she would tell him she longed to be his wife. If he wanted to be married soon, she'd suggest spending their honeymoon in the log cabin home in Kalispell. She could think of no place more perfect. A twinge of doubt assailed her. *Would Charles be equally content with a Kalispell honeymoon?* He certainly hadn't wanted her to go there in the first place.

"I'll go anywhere on earth *my wife* chooses for a honeymoon," he huskily told Patti when she faltered an acceptance of his long-standing proposal that night. "If it's Kalispell you want, it's Kalispell you'll get."

Tears of joy mingled with his kiss. They partially blurred the fierce gleam in his face, but after Charles left, she wondered. There had been far more in that look than the mere desire to please her. Patti quickly brushed the disturbing thought aside and concentrated on the many things she would have to do for the simple wedding she'd awaited for so long. Chaplain Terence O'Shea would perform the ceremony in the hospital chapel, of course. Lindsey would wear pale green and Shina yellow to set off their red and black hair, respectively. As for herself, she would be gowned in her mother's carefully preserved satin wedding gown.

She hugged her chest with her arms and ecstatically planned to telephone Dan Davis as soon as she and Charles set a date. She knew he'd made no attempt to rent the log cabin home. Had he hoped she would return?

"I am, God," she told her heavenly Father and Friend. "Only not as Dan and I discussed."

Patti couldn't make that call for some time. An unexpected cross-country flight took Charles away from Seattle for the rest of August. When he finally came home and joyously burst into her apartment, he found everything changed.

A grave-eyed Patti met him at the door. Her tear-stained face showed suffering. She gave a little cry and ran into his arms.

They closed around her. "What's happened?" he hoarsely asked.

She stared at him with unseeing eyes. "Dan Davis died this afternoon."

He relaxed. "I'm sorry, Patti, but he was an old man. Was it a heart attack?"

Patti pulled back, shocked at Charles's lack of real interest. Even though he hadn't known Dan, he knew how much she loved the old cowboy.

"No. His heart is — was as sound as mine." She shook her head, trying to clear away the fog surrounding it ever since Ma Hoff's phone call came a few hours earlier.

"Bad news about Dan," Ma tersely said. "One of those freakish things that can happen to anyone. A cottontail sprang up out of nowhere and spooked Dan's horse. The ornery cuss threw him." She paused.

Never a horse what couldn't be rode.
Never a cowpoke what couldn't be
    throwed.

The idiotic rhyme from long ago mimicked Dan's voice in Patti's brain and clutched at her throat. "How bad is he?"

"He didn't make it." Gentle sympathy flowed over the miles. "He hit his head on a rock outcropping. By the time Pa got there, Dan was dead."

"Why?" Patti whispered. "How can God let this happen, just when Dan was home and happy?"

She heard a quick-drawn breath before Ma Hoff said, "Pa and I've been asking ourselves that, Child. The only thing we can think is that if Dan had been given a choice, he'd have wanted it this way. The doctor who came out from Kalispell said he died instantly." The lengthening wire faithfully reproduced her tear-clogged voice. "He loved you, Patti. Just last night he talked about how much you reminded him of Sarah and how powerful glad he was to know you. He looked forward to seeing you again."

Patti's hand trembled until she nearly dropped the phone. "Now he won't."

Some of the sass came back to Ma Hoff's voice. "If you don't know better than that, you ought to be ashamed, Patti Thompson! Not a verse in the Bible's any clearer than John 11:26: 'And whosoever liveth and believeth in me shall never die. . . .' " Her voice softened. "Honey, Pa and I are hanging onto that promise mighty hard. You need to do the same, if you want to get past this. It would please Dan. Pa's coming in, so I'd better go. I'll let you know about the services. I'm sure we'll find Dan left something to show his wishes."

Patti stared at the silent phone long after she hung it up. Snatches of the conversation returned. Ma Hoff's unshakable faith cushioned some of the shock, and warmth stole into the nurse's heart. She had seen death many times, even blessed it when it came as a release from pain. *Thank God Dan Davis had accepted Christ long ago!* The foolish cottontail and a spooked horse had not caught him unprepared. She could almost hear him drawl, "Sarah's been waitin' for quite a spell. I'll bet she's standin' as close to heaven's window as she can get. No need for her to light a lamp for me. God's glory will be chasin' away the shadows."

Healing tears came from the mental picture of the old cowboy whose homespun wisdom had enriched Patti's life and opened her eyes to many things.

Yet she longed for the comfort of human touch and counted off the minutes until Charles arrived.

Now he had come, only to disappoint her. Where were the concern and comfort she craved? Patti searched the charming face. Admiration blazed like a forest fire in Charles's blue eyes, but they held no real understanding. Neither did his words, "I suppose this means we won't be able to spend our honeymoon in Kalispell." A curious shadow crept over his face, turning her fiancé into a stranger. A moment later his face cleared, but not before the damage had been done. It confirmed Patti's earlier suspicions. For some unknown reason,

Charles Bradley had desperately wanted to honeymoon in Kalispell.

Patti felt chilled without knowing why. "I'm very tired, Charles. If you don't mind, I need to spend some time alone." How ironic. Sending him away after she'd waited hours for him to come!

"Of course. Perhaps you'll be more like yourself tomorrow." He brushed her lips with his and stiffly marched to the door. Patti knew she had angered him but was too numb to care. *How could he have been so insensitive, so unfeeling?* Charles obviously cared more about how Dan Davis's death affected his plans than about her grief. Patti sadly stumbled to bed, feeling she had sustained not one, but two great losses.

CHAPTER 6

The simple graveside service requested in Dan Davis's papers took place without Patti. She awakened feeling dizzy and nauseated the morning she planned to fly to Montana, with a fever well over 102 degrees.

"This is ridiculous," she complained to the doctor who came to check on her. "I take my flu shots as faithfully as I brush my teeth." She staggered back to bed after letting him in.

"Last year's shot would have pretty much worn off and it isn't time for this year's," he told her sympathetically.

"I know. Whatever happened to the good old days when people had the flu in winter instead of all year round?" She coughed and grimaced. "Ouch."

"You know the drill," the doctor told her. "Rest. Drink, drink, drink — as much water and juice as you can get down. I'll have the hospital pharmacy send you something for fever when it's over one hundred degrees. I'll also have someone check on you later today. Who's your nearest neighbor?"

"April and Allison Andrews, but don't bother." Patti scrunched down in her bed. "I just want to sleep."

The doctor's eyes twinkled. "My, my, nurses do make troublesome patients," he teased, then sheepishly admitted, "my wife says I'm the world's worst patient. Being on the other side of the sheets isn't much fun." He started away then stopped. "I'll leave your door to the corridor unlocked so you won't have to get up to answer it."

"All right," Patti croaked. "If anyone bothers me, I'll breathe on them."

The doctor laughed. "No one will. The door at the far end that opens from the covered passage leading to Shepherd of Love is locked at all times."

It took too much effort to tell him she knew that. "Thanks." Something niggled at her tired brain. "Oh, could you please have someone call Mrs. Hoff in Kalispell? The number is by the phone. I was supposed to fly to Montana for a funeral service this afternoon."

"Of course."

Patti barely heard the click of the latch when he left. Pressure pushed down against the top of her head like a black cloud on a mountaintop. When she put her left hand to her cheek, the diamond engagement ring Charles had placed on her third finger dug into her cheek. Patti removed it and put it under her pillow. She drank deeply from the carafe of ice water the doctor had thoughtfully left on a small table by her bed, slept, dreamed, slept again. The pharmacy messenger came and went. Patti gobbled down her medicine and slept some more.

Hours or what seemed like eons later, the Andrews twins came in. Patti was too tired to muddle out who gave her a sponge bath and who brought a fresh sleep shirt to replace her sweaty one, then fed her broth. Refreshed, she noticed how skillfully the girls used their training in how to change a bed with a patient in it. She and Shepherd of Love were in good, capable hands. After putting her engagement ring safely away in a jewel box that held mostly costume stuff, they quietly left her to sleep again.

Patti's first real bout with influenza since childhood eventually ran its course. Yet the listlessness that followed troubled her. Why was it taking so long to recuperate? she wondered. She had seen patients cling to illness to avoid facing life. Was she doing the same? It had been heavenly peaceful in her apartment with the excuse of being contagious to avoid work and its stress, even Charles.

Realization came the morning Patti planned to report for duty. By the time she showered and dressed, the dark cloud had again descended on her. She called the Outpatient supervisor and explained she just wasn't up to coming back. Patti sank to the couch and stared at the wall, wondering what was wrong with her, vaguely dreading Charles's visit that night. Influenza did strange things, but how could it have swallowed the eagerness she normally felt at his coming? Perhaps she subconsciously knew she couldn't deal with making plans just yet. He would want to talk about their future now that she was better.

"Am I really better?" Patti wondered aloud. She pressed her hands to her head. The foreboding sensation didn't budge.

An hour later, the hospital director knocked at her door. Patti gasped. "My goodness, what are you doing here?" She felt herself turn fiery red. "I mean, you're welcome, but this is a surprise."

The keen-eyed man waited until she seated herself then dropped to a nearby chair. "I came because I suspect one of my nurses may need me."

She shouldn't have been surprised. The caring director kept his finger on the pulse of every part of Shepherd of Love, especially his employees. Weakness and gratitude sent a rush of emotion through her.

"All right, Nurse Thompson. There's more here than influenza. I received a diagnosis from your doctor of flu and extreme fatigue. What have you been doing to yourself?" He leaned back in the chair as if he had all the time in the world.

"I don't know where to begin." Her voice sounded tight, even to herself. "Maybe with last year. It wasn't a very good one."

"Tell me about it." Bit by bit, the compassionate director extracted the ups and downs in Patti's life like nut meat from a shell. By the time she finished with the grief over losing Dan Davis, she felt she'd been turned inside out.

After a long, understanding silence, the director quietly asked, "Is there somewhere you can go to get away from everything and everyone for a time? What about your parents?"

Patti shook her head. "They're retired and away on a long trip."

"If it were possible, would you be able to handle going back to Montana? To the Hoffs and Running H? They sound like good medicine. What about the log cabin in Kalispell? Would it bring back too many painful memories?"

"I don't know." Patti closed her eyes. The peace she had known in both the log cabin and at the ranch enfolded her. "All my memories from actually being there are happy. Dan — Mr. Davis hoped I would come back. He said I could use his house, even though he was moving to the Running H."

"I want you to take an extended leave of absence. If you don't go to Montana, choose another place," the director told her. "Life has been hitting you with one blow after another recently. Your body and mind are clamoring for rest. God wants you to listen to them. If you refuse to ignore what they're telling you, it may result in serious damage to your health." He patted her shoulder and smiled. "Consider yourself on leave of absence, as of now. Let me know where you're going and when you're leaving the hospital."

"I will," she promised. With the decision out of her hands, the dark cloud oppressing her miraculously lifted. Patti felt like a fraud when she ushered the caring doctor out. "Good grief," she explained to the closed door. "All it took was knowing I needed to let down. That's the first step to recovery. Now to think things over." She curled up on her comfortable couch and closed her eyes. Instead of thinking, she promptly fell asleep!

The mentally exhausted nurse awakened feeling more rested than she had in weeks. Grief at losing Dan Davis remained, but she knew healing had begun. Instead of going to the staff dining room for lunch, Patti prepared an enormous sandwich and drank a large glass of milk.

"Flat out lazy, that's what I am," she admitted with a yawn. She quickly washed her few dishes, headed back to the couch, and picked up a new inspirational novel. Sleep claimed her before she finished the first page.

Patti roused from a dream of Montana. She tried to recapture it in the delicious interval between sleep and full consciousness. Much of it eluded her, yet she remembered riding the range with the sun and wind in her face. She rode alone, but the deep rumbling laughter she would always associate with her cowboy friend sang in the air, bringing her peace. The dream changed in a flash, putting Patti in the tranquil living room of the log cabin in Kalispell. The picture of Sarah McClelland Davis welcomed her, as she felt it had weeks earlier. Only now Sarah's face glowed with far more joy and her eyes shone with happiness.

Patti came fully awake. *What an odd dream!* She lay still and considered it. According to her beliefs, even now Dan and Sarah were reunited in the presence of the One they had loved and served so long and faithfully. Patti felt at peace.

"I know there will be times when a certain laugh, or song, or the way the wind blows will catch me off guard and I'll come unglued," she soberly told her heavenly Father. "I also know each time will be a little easier. Lord, is it Your will for me to go to Montana?"

She waited a long time. No thunder or lightning replied. God didn't speak in the mighty roar of a storm. Patti waited a little longer, then rose from the couch. She took out the painting of the cabin she had done using yellow for the cottonwood leaves and propped it up on a table. Nostalgia clutched at her heart. She could almost see Dan Davis opening the door and welcoming her home.

Her heartbeat increased. "Lord, is this my answer? This feeling of rightness?"

No still, small voice sounded. Yet the rest

in Patti's soul gave answer enough. Eager to start the wheels of her going in motion, she reached for the phone. The Hoffs would either know about the log cabin's availability or be able to tell her whom to contact. To her dismay, the phone rang a dozen times. She started to cradle it, then heard the breathless, welcome voice of Ma Hoff.

"Hello?"

Memories overwhelmed Patti, leaving her weak. "Ma? It's Patti Thompson," she said in a small voice.

"My goodness, you sound faraway! I know you are, but it's not a very clear connection. Shall I call you back?"

Patti cleared her throat and raised her voice. "Can you hear me now?"

"I sure can. How are you feeling? We've been worried about you."

"That's why I'm calling. I'm over the flu, but the doctors say I need a long rest. Is there any chance I can rent Dan's Kalispell cabin?"

Ma Hoff sounded doubtful. "I really don't know. The lawyer who handles things told Pa things would be settled before long. For heaven's sake, don't wait until then, Child. Your room here's ready and waiting, just as you left it. You can stay as long as you like. Pa and I are rattling around this old ranch-house like the last two beans in a stewpot since Dan moved on."

Moved on. What a typical, range-like way to describe death!

"You're sure I won't be in the way?"

"Land sakes, no! How soon can you come? We will pick you up at the airport."

"I'll have to let you know." Patti choked up again. "Thanks, Ma. Pa, too."

"Don't thank us. We miss our kitchen flunky something fierce." The warm-hearted rancher's wife quickly said good-bye and hung up.

For the first time in days, Patti's former enthusiasm sparked. A moment later, it went out, drowned by a flood of apprehension. *What would Charles say?* She glanced at her watch and turned the engagement ring she'd put back in its proper place around and around. She wouldn't have to wait long to find out. In a few hours, he'd swoop down on her the way hawks do on defenseless baby chicks.

"What's wrong with you, Patti Thompson?" she cried. "You've promised to marry Charles. How can you make such an odious comparison?" She pushed aside all thought of going to the dining room and stared at the four walls until she felt like climbing them. April and Allison Andrews ran in for a few minutes, but tactfully left when Charles arrived.

He had never looked more handsome than in his well-cut gray slacks and a soft blue shirt that matched his eyes.

"Darling!" Charles held out his arms the moment the twins disappeared. "I've missed you so much."

Patti relaxed in the security of his arms. How foolish she had been to let illness build up dread! This was Charles, the man she loved, the man with whom she planned to spend her life until death separated them.

For the first half hour, everything went well. Although Charles had kept in touch by phone and sent enough flowers to decorate a wedding chapel and reception, he acted as though they'd been out of touch for years. At last he said, "Now that you're feeling better, we can make plans. I've arranged to have the entire month of December off for our honeymoon. How about a wedding just after Thanksgiving?" He laughed a satisfied laugh. "I'll be the one giving thanks!"

Patti took a deep breath. "I–I'm not sure it will work out."

"Excuse me?" He drew back, looking as if he'd been slapped.

"The doctors are putting me on a leave of

absence for an indefinite period of time. Would you believe the hospital director himself came to check on me?"

She managed a weak laugh. "Seems I've been getting myself so run down I'm not much good to either the hospital or myself. They're sending me away."

"Where? When?" His words cracked like a lightning-struck Ponderosa pine.

"To Montana, as soon as possible."

Charles's mouth set in a grim line. "Impossible! I can't get away now."

"You don't have to get away. The Hoffs want me to come stay with them, at least until Mr. Davis's estate is settled. After that, I want to rent the log cabin." She tried to overcome the fluttering in her throat and sound enthusiastic. "I'll have time for a long rest, which is the doctors' prescription. I can't imagine not being well enough to marry by the end of November, Charles, but I won't make a promise I may not be able to keep."

Rage contorted his handsome face. "Well, isn't this sweet. I go through the red tape of obtaining an entire month off of work and you tell me it's all in vain."

Some of Patti's spunk returned. "I didn't plan to get sick, you know."

"You probably wouldn't have, if you'd

stayed here when I wanted you to, instead of gallivanting off to Montana with some broken-down ex-cowboy!"

"You call an all-expense-paid vacation and making an old man happy for a couple of weeks gallivanting?" Patti curbed her rising anger and tried for the light touch. "Them's fightin' words, pardner."

Wrong move. It touched off Charles Bradley like a match to tinder. "You are not going back to Kalispell. Period. Think I'll take the chance of —" He broke off. "I forbid it. You look fine to me except for being a little pale, which is to be expected. If you have to get away, go to the ocean or mountains, not Montana."

Patti made a desperate grab for the reins of her slipping control. She missed. "May I inquire what medical school issued your diploma, Dr. Bradley?" she asked in a tone that should have warned him. Instead, it pushed him farther over the edge.

"I hate sarcasm in women, so you may as well stop it right there," he ranted.

Patti had observed the miracle of cataract patients with their sight restored.

She had rejoiced with them, yet had never known the full measure of their clear vision until now. Charles's ultimatum was more effective than laser surgery. All Patti's nebulous doubts and fears sprang into full-fledged knowledge. They removed a far more dangerous blindness than not being able to physically see: blindness formed by her loneliness and mistaking attraction for lasting love. Life with Charles would be a hearth of fire.

"Well?" He gripped her shoulders, as he had done once before.

This time Patti did not wrench free. She simply said, "Take your hands off me, Charles. Get out and don't come back."

"You don't mean that." He attempted to draw her to him, but she stiffened.

"I never meant anything more in my life. I won't link my life with someone who tramples and doesn't respect me. You don't want a wife. You want a possession. I'm sorry I didn't recognize it sooner."

Charles freed her and crossed his arms. An ugly expression darkened his face.

"You may as well stop trying to get your own way. That's all it is, you know. I don't plan to fall for it. No woman is ever going to rule me. I'm leaving, but I'll be back when you've come to your senses."

Patti stripped off the engagement ring that had changed from a symbol of love to one of servitude and held it out.

"I meant what I said. Good-bye, Charles."

He laughed in her face and warded her off when she tried to drop it in his shirt pocket.

"Oh, no, you don't! I bought this for you and you're going to wear it. I never give up anything that's mine. Meaning you."

"Take it or leave it. I don't care. Once you go, I won't be responsible for the ring. I'm leaving soon." A burst of independence made her add, "Since I have no idea when or even if I'll be back, I'm giving up this place." It was a new idea, born of necessity, but it was a good one, she knew. "I'll store what I don't take with me. You probably won't want the ring left lying around in an empty apartment."

Charles sullenly accepted it but not an iota of defeat showed in his face.

"You'll be back." He raised an eyebrow. "I can't guarantee I'll still be available. I know a dozen women who'd be glad to accept me, with or without a ring. Sailors aren't the only ones with girls in every port, you know."

"Thank you," Patti quietly told him. "If I still had lingering doubts about you, that last despicable sentence erased them forever." She flung open the outside door. "Are you leaving, or must I call Security?"

He slouched out, head high. Anyone seeing him wouldn't guess in a million years the woman he professed to love had just dumped him. Patti watched him stride to his car, his "hail-the-conquering-hero" attitude intact. It made her feel better about the hideous scene. Her sharp rejection may have nicked Charles Bradley's pride, but it hadn't even come close to wounding his heart.

Would he accept her edict as final? Patti shook her head. Only the most conceited man on earth would believe any decent woman would take him back after that vile threat. Yet Charles's comment that he never gave up anything he wanted sent chills through her.

What would she do if she were him? "Stay away for a few days to teach me a lesson so I'd come crawling back," she decided. "Good! By the time he decides to honor me with his presence again, I'll be in Kalispell. Horrors! What if he follows me? He knows the Hoffs' names and the name of the ranch.

"Forget it and get busy," she commanded herself. "God can take care of you just as well in Montana as here." A wave of gratitude washed over her. "Thanks, Lord. You haven't showed me all of Your will in my life, but You certainly showed me just now Charles Bradley isn't part of it!"

Patti accomplished so much in such a short time, it amazed even her. She made plane reservations. A quick call to Chaplain and Lindsey O'Shea resulted in willing permission for Patti to store anything she liked at their farmhouse near Redmond. Lindsey had a day off, so she and Terence brought boxes and insisted on doing the packing while Patti supervised. Shina Ito Hyde and the Andrews twins came after day shift ended.

√"You could at least have given us enough notice to throw a farewell party," Shina complained over the take-out chicken dinners her husband, Kevin, obligingly picked up and brought to the willing workers.

"We'll miss you, but you need a change, Pal. At least for now," Lindsey added. "Just don't forget us."

"Fat chance." Patti knew if she responded as seriously as her friends looked, the parting would be all sorrow and *not* sweet. She forced down a bite of potatoes and gravy wondering why it didn't stick on the lump in her throat.

"Okay," Terence said a little later. "You have what you're taking on the plane. We ship the boxes marked with an X and store the rest. Right?"

"Right." Patti secretly wished they would all just leave. One by one they did, with the frankly envious Andrews twins last. Patti avoided looking at the empty apartment. Doing so meant remembering how many years she had spent at Shepherd of Love. What did God have in mind for her? A leave of absence, or a whole new life?

Too weary to worry about it, Patti went to bed and didn't waken until her alarm sounded. An hour later, she stepped into the taxi she had insisted on taking to the airport. She simply couldn't handle lingering farewells at the airport.

"Good-bye, Mount Rainier, hello Montana," she saluted the snow-capped peak. Chin up, face forward, Patti Thompson flew into a future known only to God.

CHAPTER 7

Scott Sloan grabbed his denim jacket and stepped from the white Bell Jet-Ranger. *Another mission successfully accomplished,* he thought. Scott took off his black baseball cap and ruefully stared at the dirty helicopter. Dust streaks partially obscured its red markings and large red cross painted on the side.

"Not bad, considering where we've been." The nurse who had ridden beside him grinned. "Still identifiable, though."

"Yeah. Everyone in Kalispell knows the Parker Rescue Service choppers."

"As well as the miraculous feats Scott Sloan and his fellow pilots accomplish in getting expert help — such as mine — to those who need it," the nurse teased. She smirked at her double-sided compliment and headed for the hangar.

Scott paused long enough to give the chopper a surreptitious pat. The warm glow he always experienced after returning to Kalispell from a flight saturated him and a rare smile surfaced. Scott stretched his tall, lean body. Muscles rippled under the black turtleneck. It felt good to be home, even though home meant a strictly masculine apartment not far from the flying field. How different from the home he and the nurse who had accompanied him had left a short time ago! The rude cabin perched on a grassy knoll that overlooked an isolated, wooded draw. It shouted the fact it had been built with enthusiasm, furnished with love.

Mike Parker often raged at people who chose to live so far from towns where they had limited access to doctors, even while providing medical support. Scott admired their pluck. The young couple in the cabin reminded him of the countless intrepid pioneers who forged homes in the wilderness after crossing thousands of weary miles on foot or in covered wagons. If he married, perhaps he and his wife would be one of them.

Scott's smile faded. A mouth that shouted its owner had known tragedy and suffering tightened. Long, denim-clad legs carried him to the hangar. He found the flight service owner receiving an official report of the follow-up call. A few days earlier, Scott

116

had flown a doctor to the cabin after a frantic call from the wife. Her husband had been felling a tree. In one of the hazardous twists of logging, it veered. A widow maker crashed down on the man.

"He's stunned, but conscious. He has a deep gash on his arm and something wrong with one ankle," the wife said. "I don't want to move him. I'm also afraid to bring him in our vehicle over all the rough miles between here and a doctor."

The hurry-up call resulted in a neat stitching job done on the spot. The man's leg proved to be sprained, not broken, and the victim showed no signs of concussion. The patient and the plucky girl-wife refused to be flown to Kalispell after the doctor admitted there was little need. Today's check-up showed husband and wife were both doing well.

"Anything to add?" the round-faced owner asked Scott when the nurse finished.

It amused Scott. His boss never failed to ask, even though all three knew the pilot wouldn't have anything more than what the nurse or doctor reported. Scott shook his head.

"Another happy ending."

"Also another happy landing," the nurse pertly told him.

Scott felt himself congeal. Nausea rose in him. He covered with a laugh, turned on his heel, and left the hangar as rapidly as possible, hoping to cover his reaction. It didn't work.

"What's wrong with Stone Face?" he heard the nurse ask. Scott knew she wasn't being sarcastic, just concerned. He flinched just the same. Gratitude replaced some of the sick feeling when Mike replied, "He gets that way when he's hungry. Speaking of which, my wife's going to have my head if I don't get out of here on time. I've kept supper waiting the last three nights."

"Ah, the life of a busy man."

Scott could hear them good-naturedly wrangling even after he climbed in his Jeep. He buried his throbbing head in his hands and waited for the feeling to subside. He refused to drive until it did. No one so churned up inside had the right to menace others by being on the highway.

His rapid heartbeat slowed perceptibly. Scott rejoiced. It took less time now than in former years and months. If only the thrusts from his past would give warning! They never did. He couldn't tell what might set him off. For a long time after the incident that changed him from laughing pilot to Stone Face, he had worried about what

118

might happen if a flashback caught him in the sky. Only once had shattering memories attacked while on a flight. Intense prayer to the God he had known since childhood helped him overcome that particular fear.

Remembering that day sponged away the last of Scott's trauma, at least for this time. He had never told another living human being about the day cold sweat broke out on his forehead and threatened him with helplessness. He had been flying alone, sent back to base by a nurse who decided she needed a doctor for a patient she didn't want moved.

Exactly what triggered the flashbacks, Scott never knew. He only knew he cried for help at the moment fear began to engulf him. The answer came in a way he didn't expect. A way he knew the world would scorn. Even after all this time, Scott could almost feel the gentle pressure of hands covering his own wet and shaking ones. And the peace that had fallen over him like the diaphanous wedding veil on a bride.

Never again had he experienced the recall while flying. Episodes grew more and more infrequent, just as the rough but caring military doctor promised years ago. Today was the first in months.

"Thanks, God," Scott muttered. "Someday, I may be able to go back and thank the doctor, too. I wonder if he'd believe me?"

Confidence restored, he considered the idea on the way to his apartment. A quick check of the nearly empty refrigerator drew the corners of his mouth down. He'd eat out and shop on the way home. A pang of envy for the meal Mike Parker would find ready and waiting filled him. Scott shook his head. Until he could break chains from the past, he wouldn't inflict himself on any woman. Marriage was a tough proposition, especially in these days. Two broken people couldn't make one whole person.

A piquant face danced in the air before Scott while he showered and changed. Odd that he should think of the pretty blond nurse who had come from Seattle weeks ago. She must have a lot of the right stuff in her, or she wouldn't have taken time to drive Dan Davis home to Montana. Maybe she had an ulterior motive. Dan had to be pretty well off, after selling the Running H. Was Patti Thompson a gold-digger, out for what she could get from the lonely old ex-cowboy she'd cared for? She had certainly charmed Mike Parker, so much he offered her a job. God forbid. The last thing he needed was an opportunist worming her way into everyone's good graces in order to cash in on Dan's holdings.

The thought depressed Scott. He hastily pulled on his boots and strode out to the Jeep. Patti Thompson hadn't looked like a gold-digger. There had been something in her eyes. Scott couldn't exactly describe it, but it reminded him of the trapped look in the eyes of a wounded deer he'd once seen in the forest.

He snorted. "There's no guarantee I'd know a gold-digger if I saw one. I doubt they look like old-time dance hall floozies. At least the nurse doesn't." His comparison brought a grin. Yet after a substantial supper, the thoughtful pilot turned his Jeep toward Dan's log cabin home. The nurse would be long gone and it felt like a century since Scott had dropped in on Dan.

Disappointment far beyond finding no one home smote Scott when he reached the log cabin. Although light filtered through the drawn shades, a sense of emptiness surrounded the place. Repeated ringing of the doorbell brought no response.

"Dan's gone and lights are on a timer," Scott surmised. "Too bad."

He saw the old man for a few minutes after church the following Sunday. Scott learned the cowboy had "packed up his duds and hied himself out" to the Running

H. "The Hoffs found out they needed my help in runnin' the ranch," Dan added. His faded blue eyes held more color than Scott had seen in some time. So did his tanned cheeks. The pilot congratulated him and promised to drop by as soon as he could find time. He started to ask about Patti Thompson but thought better of it. Long experience with well-meaning friends who leaped at the chance to play matchmaker silenced him. The most casual inquiry would be more than enough to bring a cackle from Dan Davis and a gleam into Ma Hoff's eye!

A busier than usual schedule for the next few weeks shoved everything out of Scott's mind except flying, eating, and sleeping. He missed church, something he hated doing. It couldn't be helped. A rash of incidents with tourists kept the entire staff of the Rescue Service on the go. Summer cooled into fall and Scott still hadn't made it out to the ranch.

One afternoon Mike Parker received a call. Scott lounged in a chair in the office. He saw Mike's usually jovial face sag.

"When? How bad?" He paused. "I'll send Scott and a doctor." He banged down the receiver, looking strangely shrunken. "Get ready for a trip out to the Running H."

Scott bounded from his chair. "Who's hurt?"

Mike shook his head and licked his lips. "Dan Davis. It's worse than hurt."

"Dead?"

"Hoff says so. We'll send a doctor, anyway." Parker dialed one of the doctors they called on for emergency trips and tersely explained the situation.

Scott shook his head to clear it.

"How'd it happen?" he demanded when Mike hung up. "I haven't seen Dan for weeks, but he looked fine when I did."

"Horse spooked and pitched him headfirst onto a rock pile," Mike said heavily. "It happens." He leaned back until his chair squeaked. "At least, we know where he's gone. Dan Davis was not only a top hand and rancher, but a real Christian."

"Yeah." Scott reached for his baseball cap and shoved it down on his dark hair. "We'll miss him."

The doctor said the same thing when they reached the Running H.

"Died instantly," he confirmed. "Hard on those of us who liked and respected him, but quick and easy, the way Dan would choose to go." He gestured toward the rolling hills rising to distant tree-covered mountains.

"He also spent his last days out here where he belonged," Scott added. "We can be thankful for that." He smiled at the Hoffs. "I'm just sorry I didn't get to see him again."

"He understood. Dan never was one to put pleasure ahead of business. He knew you'd come when you could," Pa Hoff gruffly said.

Scott and the doctor climbed into the chopper and started back to Kalispell.

They reported in to Mike, who asked Scott if he had anything to add, as usual. Scott didn't, also as usual. Instead of leaving, he slumped back in the chair.

"Something eating you, Stone Face?" Mike wanted to know.

"No. Just thinking how much good Dan did during his life."

The round face beneath the balding head brightened. "He sure did. Half of Kalispell will show up for his funeral, or whatever kind of service he wanted."

"I'll bet the Bell Jet-Ranger it won't be fancy."

Mike chuckled. "No bets! Dan wouldn't stand for any such affair. Think that nurse, Patti Thompson isn't it, will show? It's a long way from Seattle, but she seemed to think a lot of Dan."

A funny little sensation ran through Scott. He'd been wondering the same thing.

"She might." He didn't add his earlier suspicions about her. Best not to judge. Time had a way of proving a person right or wrong.

"Dan really hoped she'd come back." Mike leaned forward and grew confidential. "He told her she could live in his log cabin home any time, even though he'd moved back to the Running H."

"He did!" Fresh suspicion poured over Scott like a deluge of ice water. "How do you know?"

"He told me. Said he'd appreciate it if I'd give her a job if she took him up on it." Mike looked reflective. "Wouldn't be a bad idea. Some of our nurses are wanting to cut down on trips." He laughed. "I don't suppose she'll ever come. Not many gals are interested in giving up the city lights."

They might if they knew they would benefit financially. Scott kept the unpleasant thought to himself. Again, time would prove what kind of person a certain Patti Thompson really was.

The simple graveside service Dan had left instructions to hold didn't attract quite half of Kalispell, as Mike Parker predicted.

125

However, the large crowd included most of the churchgoers, ranch families, cowboys, and leading citizens of the area. The minister spoke simply and effectively. No one present would leave the service without knowing the way to salvation.

"It's what Dan wanted," Ma Hoff whispered to Scott, who stood beside her. "He said the last and best thing he could do for folks was make clear the path they'd have to ride if they aimed to get to heaven."

Scott nodded, wanting to ask why Patti Thompson hadn't come, but hesitant.

Mike Parker had no such qualms. When the service ended, he shook hands with the Hoffs and said, "I thought maybe Dan's nurse friend would be here."

"She planned to fly in this morning, but woke up so sick she had to have a doctor from Shepherd of Love Hospital where she works call and say she wasn't coming," Pa Hoff told them.

Scott skeptically wondered if she were really sick. She probably was, since a doctor had called. According to Dan Davis, Shepherd of Love hired only strong Christians, not personnel who would lie. He tried to shrug off a feeling of loss. If he never saw her again, so what?

"We're hoping Patti will come for Christmas," Ma Hoff put in. "She lost some of her forlorn look last summer when she stayed with us. Besides, her folks are retired and away on some kind of long trip."

Scott fought the instant change in his mood. He had no place for love in his life. Patti Thompson still might be a gold-digger. He shored up his defenses, but Ma Hoff's choice of the word "forlorn" wore away at them as water does on rock. Evidently he hadn't been the only one to sense trouble in the nurse's eyes.

"Pa and I are going to be a mite lonely." Ma laughed. "Well, as lonely as life on a cattle ranch lets us. Come see us when you can, Scott."

"I will." He took her hand in his, then shook her husband's. "Things should settle down soon. At least I hope they will." He drove his Jeep back to town determined to keep his promise soon. In the meantime, he vowed to keep in touch by phone. "If a person's too busy for their friends, then they're too busy, period," Scott's father used to say.

Scott winced. For the past several years, he had been guilty of doing just that. Something teased at his mind. It niggled until he reached his apartment and took down a dog-eared copy of the anthology

Poems That Touch the Heart. He opened it to the first page and read "Around the Corner," the haunting words written by Charles Hanson Towne.

The poem spoke of one whose friend lived just around the corner. The narrator shared that his friend knew he thought as much of him as in the days before the busy world kept them apart. Again and again, the narrator planned to go see his friend. He didn't. One day a telegram came telling him his friend had died. He had put off visiting one day too many.

Scott closed the book. *Had Towne experienced what he wrote?* It would account for the poignancy of the poem. How fitting for Scott Sloan's life, as well. Because of work and regret, he had not only put off going to see friends, he had shut the door between them. No wonder he had earned the name Stone Face.

In the beginning, it had seemed the only thing to do. He couldn't bear the stumbling assurances of friendship, the shock in the faces of even his most trusted friends. He eagerly seized the opportunity to fly for Mike Parker and get away from everyone and everything he knew. In order to be fair, he told Mike as much of the story as his future boss needed to know.

Scott hadn't forgotten the paunchy man's response. First, a keen gaze bore into him, testing him. Then he asked, "Are you sure of what you've told me?"

Scott's stomach muscles twisted. "Before God, I wish I weren't!"

A long silence followed, broken by Mike's raspy voice. "The way I figure it, a man's past is past. I don't see that you did anything dishonorable." He held up his hand when Scott would have protested. "It all depends on where you're standing, Sloan. All I want to know is, can you do the job I need done?"

Back on secure ground, Scott squared his shoulders under his lightweight jacket. His head went up in the fearless manner that once characterized him to those in his command. Flying, both fixed-wing and helicopter, was something he did and did well. "I can." He drew in a deep, troubled breath but met the watching gaze without flinching. "The only thing is, my references are checkered."

Mike shuffled the papers Scott had presented at the beginning of the interview. So far Parker had ignored them. "Why didn't you give me only the ones praising you?"

"It wouldn't be honest." Scott's jaw clenched. So much for securing the job.

He unzipped the tight line of his mouth

enough to say, "Sir, I have to answer to God and live with myself. I can't withhold any information that will affect my job performance. It's all there. What isn't there is personal."

"Good enough. Are we ready to discuss salary, hours, that kind of thing?"

Scott felt as if he'd been hit with a lightning bolt. "You haven't read the reports."

"I've always been a good judge of men. I'll take you on trust."

Scott didn't waver by an iota. "I prefer you read my papers first."

A curious expression crossed the flight service owner's face. He scanned the pages so rapid-fire Scott knew Mike had either taken a speed-reading course or couldn't care less what they contained.

"Now if you'll slap a more cheerful expression on that stone face of yours, we'll talk about salary and hours. Right now you look like a cat that ate a sour mouse!" Parker's hand shot out.

Scott grabbed it with the desperation with which a cowboy bucked off into the middle of a stampede snatches for a partner's extended hand. The first real laugh he'd had in months burst forth. Along with the laugh came hope he had thought dead and buried. It also brought unbounded respect for a man who judged others by what was in himself, rather than words on a page. They had been friends ever since.

True to his promise, Scott began to reach out. Instead of rushing from church, he stayed for potlucks or to visit unless he had to work. He had long since settled the question of working on the Lord's Day by following Jesus' example.

And a man with a shriveled hand was there [in the synagogue]. Looking for a reason to accuse Jesus, they asked him, "Is it lawful to heal on the Sabbath?"

He said to them, "If any of you has a sheep and it falls into a pit on the Sabbath, will you not take hold of it and lift it out?

"How much more valuable is a man than a sheep! Therefore it is lawful to do good on the Sabbath."

Then he said to the man, "Stretch out your hand." So he stretched it out and it was completely restored, just as sound as the other. Matthew 12:10–13

Sickness, accidents, and folks in need couldn't schedule emergencies. Like Jesus, when a need arose on the Sabbath, the

Rescue Service met it. The Master had not deferred help and left people to suffer. Neither would they.

CHAPTER 8

Every mile that transported Patti Thompson farther away from Seattle and closer to Kalispell brought the tired nurse a little more peace. She knew the first few moments seeing the Hoffs without Dan Davis and his broad smile in the background would be hard. However, the warmth of the ranch couple's welcome quickly dried her eyes. So did Ma Hoff's hearty hug and Pa's firm handshake.

"We're mighty proud to have you," he told her.

"We'll get you fattened up and back doing chores in the whisk of a lamb's tail," Ma promised, after a hasty examination of Patti's pale face.

"Lambs on a cattle ranch? My goodness, how the West has changed!"

Patti's temporary sadness fled in the laugh that followed. Her sense of loss returned when she glanced at the log cabin Dan had

133

occupied the last weeks of his life. However, Ma wisely bustled her guest into the house, helped her unpack her clothes, and set her to peeling vegetables for stew.

"Best thing for a body is to keep busy," the kitchen philosopher said. "How is your drawing and painting coming? Dan told us you were quite a hand at it."

"I'm glad you mentioned Dan," Patti impulsively said. "So many people won't talk about those who–who have gone on."

"Land sakes, why not?" Ma's eyebrows shot up until they almost touched her graying hair. "Seems to me doing that makes it like they never lived." Her hands stilled from beating her biscuit dough and she waved a sticky spoon. "Far as Pa and I are concerned, Dan's more alive and a whole lot happier now than he ever was. It would be a pure shame to pack his memories away like my mother used to pack winter woolens in mothballs."

Patti laughed at the comparison. The Hoffs' homespun humor never failed to delight her. She looked around the spacious kitchen and inwardly purred with satisfaction. Except for Dan Davis's absence, it was as if the troubled time between her leaving and returning to the Running H never existed. Patti glanced at her ring finger. Not even the trace of a white mark showed the brief time Charles Bradley's diamond ring had circled it. She shivered. Thank God for her narrow escape! What if she had married Charles and been subject to his rages? Or worse? His boast about other women showed him incapable of fidelity.

Ma Hoff's keen eyes missed nothing. "Are you cold, Child?"

"No. I'm thanking God I'm here." Patti hesitated, then in a few well-chosen sentences informed the older woman what had happened in Seattle.

"My grandmother would say it's a good thing you're shut of him," Ma said.

"What if he follows me?" Another shiver chased up her spine. "Charles knows about the Running H. We talked about asking Dan if we could spend our honeymoon in his log cabin home." Patti made a face. "Ugh! How could I have been so mistaken about him?" She didn't add it was the second time her intuition had failed because of a handsome male face and charming manner.

"Most of us get taken in by a two-legged critter at one time or another," Ma dryly observed. "I hate to mention more practical things, but if you don't get back to your peeling, dinner will be a long time coming!"

Patti grinned. "Okay, Boss." Curiosity

made her add, "Did you?"

"What? Get taken in? Oh, sure." Ma beat her dough more furiously than ever. "Long before I met Pa, I planned to marry someone else. He went off and found a new girl. Like to broke my heart." Her eyes twinkled. " 'Course the little rascal was only eight and I was six when we got engaged."

Patti gasped and laughed until her sides ached. Life on the Running H would never prove dull with Ma Hoff around to tell stories!

The next Sunday at church, folks greeted Patti like a long lost sister. The minister made a special point of welcoming her from the pulpit. Mike Parker beamed. Patti caught a glimpse of Scott Sloan across the church. He nodded and went back to turning pages in his songbook. Patti chastised herself for caring. She'd just run away from one man. The last thing she needed was another to complicate her life. She had to concentrate on regaining her usual excellent health so she could again be of service to others.

Patti turned her attention to Pastor Hill, the middle-aged shepherd of this particular flock of worshippers. He had a knack of enlivening his sermons with vivid stories. Today was no different.

"The Bible tells us in Mark 12:31 and several other places to love our neighbors as ourselves. What kind of world would it be if everyone loved those around them *more* than themselves?" He paused and scanned the congregation.

"A legend tells of two brothers who worked a large field together and planned to share the grain when harvested.

"One brother had a wife and children. One lived alone on the other side of a hill. At harvest, the single brother said, 'I have only myself to care for. My brother needs much more than I.' Each night he filled a large sack and smuggled it into his brother's barn.

"The married brother told himself, 'I have children to care for me when I am old. My brother does not.' He also secretly carried grain to his brother's barn.

" 'How strange,' both thought. 'I give away, yet my grain is abundant as ever!'

"One night on their pilgrimage, the brothers met each other. They shouted with laughter and embraced when they saw each other's sacks of grain.

"According to legend, God was pleased with the brothers. He said the place where they met was holy. There His temple should be built. Solomon's temple is said to stand on that spot."

What an example of selflessness! Patti opened her songbook and joined in singing, "Bringing in the Sheaves," rejoicing along with the writer of the beloved words. How lighthearted she felt! She sneaked a glance across at Scott Sloan. This time he gave her a faint smile. He also took time after church to say, "It's nice to have you here again. Great sermon, wasn't it?" Yet the look in his eyes warned Scott was reserving judgment of her for some unknown reason.

"It's wonderful to be here," she frankly told him.

Mike Parker pushed up to them. "How long are you staying? What's chances of your doing some work for me? My flying nurses are complaining they don't get enough time off." His Santa Claus stomach shook when he laughed.

"Miss Thompson's been sick. Give her time to rest before shoving her into a helicopter," Scott said sharply. He turned on his heel and strode down the church aisle the same way he'd done last summer when Patti first met him.

"Well, I never!" Ma Hoff stared after him then back at Mike. "He's right. This young lady isn't doing any flying until I get some meat on her bones."

"Sorry." The rescue service owner had the grace to look ashamed. However, his bouncy personality didn't keep him down long. He winked at Patti. "If you don't call me, I'll call you. You have a job when you're ready." He walked off.

Scott Sloan slammed into his Jeep feeling like a fool. *What possessed me to protest against Mike railroading Patti Thompson into a job? She could take care of herself, couldn't she?*

"I don't want or need some out-of-condition nurse who'll fold if we get in a tight situation," he muttered. The defense fell apart like a cardboard sword. Why not admit his concern over the nurse's pale face and obvious weight loss had little to do with her ability to perform rescue work? When Patti glanced across the church, the shadow in her eyes called forth a chivalrous desire to protect her.

"She may not need it," Scott reminded himself on his way home. "That clear, blue gaze of hers could be camouflage. Folks will find it hard to believe her motives are anything but sincere." *Were they?* Surface evidence pointed to the fact she had been sick and come to Montana to rest. Scott shrugged and told himself for the umpteenth time to forget about Patti Thompson. Her motives meant nothing in his scheme of life, did they? He had a good job. He helped people, not with sacks of grain, but through his flying. Why borrow trouble?

Leaves changed color and swirled into red and yellow blizzards. Nights crisped and spread frost. Scott returned from a visit to his parents in Salt Lake City and learned two pieces of news that rocked his world.

Mike Parker announced Patti Thompson was fit for duty and ready to fly.

And, Dan Davis's probated will disclosed he had left ten thousand dollars each to the Hoffs and the church. Everything else went to the nurse from Shepherd of Love.

All Scott's earlier suspicions came back. *No wonder she had been so eager to drive Dan home!* He tightened his lips and prayed he wouldn't have Patti in his chopper. He couldn't very well ask Mike to schedule her with one of the other pilots. Yet he rebelled at the thought of flying and working with a girl who had turned out to be a common gold-digger, taking advantage of her position as a nurse in order to inherit Dan's considerable estate. *Despicable!*

"I have to hand it to her," Scott bitterly admitted. "She's clever."

He was amazed to discover others felt differently. The Hoffs lamented the fact they'd be losing Patti to a home of her own, but loyally insisted they were glad.

Mike Parker thought only of his rescue service.

"Now she'll stay," he exulted. "Maybe that's why Dan did it. He hoped she'd come back and work with us. Said she was just the kind of nurse we and those we serve need."

Scott didn't have the heart to remind his boss and friend that Patti might well sell the log home, take Dan's money from the sale of the ranch, and vamoose. He also wondered why he felt so let down. Hadn't he suspected all along there was more behind the innocent face than others saw? He firmly determined to stay as far away from the scheming little double-crosser as possible.

Patti stared across the massive desk in the lawyer's office. Had she heard him right? Yes, for he patiently repeated she had just inherited a log cabin home, a Ford Bronco, and more money than she could accumulate in a lifetime of hard work as a nurse.

"Why me?" she demanded. "Surely Mr. Davis's holdings should go to someone closer. I'm just a nurse who happened to be on duty when he came to Shepherd of Love." She shook her head. "It's too much like a fairy tale. Or something out of a novel."

"It does happen in real life," the lawyer told her.

"What if I refuse it?"

Disapproval oozed from the stern man. "Why would you do that?"

"I don't know." Patti looked at him appealingly. "It just doesn't seem real."

He relaxed. "Mr. Davis made no provision for your turning down the bequest. He said this letter would explain everything." He handed her a white envelope. "Would you like to read it before signing the papers?" His laugh made him seem more human and less an efficient, remote machine. "Turning over property, including land and bank assets, requires a great deal of paperwork." He rose. "Perhaps you'd rather be alone when you read Dan's letter."

"Yes, please," Patti gratefully said.

He smiled and went out. The door closed behind him. The ticking of the wall clock ponderously counting off time sounded loud in the quiet office.

Patti slit the sealed envelope and took out a single sheet of paper. The strong writing she knew from Dan's rare communications between Kalispell and Seattle blurred her vision. She impatiently brushed mist from her eyes and focused on the letter. Dan had spelled the words correctly, yet the letter sounded so much like him, Patti could hear his drawl and dropping g's at the end of his words.

Dear Patti,

By the time you read this, whenever it may be, I'll have moved on to a bigger, better range. You already know I'm raring to go. Sarah's waiting. Don't waste a passel of time in tears. You probably have a long life ahead of you, but looking from God's view, it won't be long before we meet again.

There's a couple of things I have to say. You're one spunky gal. You may balk like a mule about accepting what I'm leaving you. Don't. I want to know what the Good Lord's blessed me with is left in capable hands. If you don't hanker to settle in Kalispell permanent-like, sell the log cabin to someone who won't be likely to cut down my cottonwoods and spoil the place. Scott Sloan, maybe. He's a fine man and he always liked it.

The other thing's been on my mind a lot

since you left. Remember what I said about joining up your life with the wrong man. Better to ride lonesome than be in double-harness with a no-good who'll break your heart.

I sent one of the sketches you left behind to an artist feller I used to know. He wrote back all excited. He said you need training, which we both knew. He also said you have a certain something in your work that needs to be developed. It made me scratch my head, but I never did figure out exactly what he meant. At least it sounds promising. You'll have enough with what I left to take time off and find out.

Vaya con Dios, meaning "Go with God."

Your old cowboy friend,

Dan

Patti gently refolded the letter and put it in the envelope. She would treasure it forever, even more than all the material things she had inherited. The lawyer had been right. The message tore down barriers to accepting what had been given in friendship. No, in love, forged during the short time she had known Dan Davis.

Absorbed in her own thoughts, Patti didn't hear the door open.

"Miss Thompson?" The lawyer stepped

back into the room. "I trust you found Dan's message satisfactory. Are you ready to sign the papers?" He sat down behind his desk in an attitude of waiting.

"It would be wrong not to accept what he left me," Patti humbly said. "The way he put it, my inheritance is a sacred trust."

A gleam of satisfaction brightened the watching eyes. "That's how Dan hoped you'd see it. I didn't read your letter, of course, but my client and I talked about you. A lot."

Patti squirmed. "I always feel uncomfortable when someone tells me that."

"No need to, in this case," the lawyer brusquely told her. "Now about your signature . . ." He took the top page from a sheaf of documents.

By the time she finished signing, Patti's head spun. Dan Davis had chosen his legal representative well. The lawyer meticulously explained each paper and faithfully asked if she had questions before going on to the next. At last they finished. "It will take a little more time to get everything transferred into your name," he said. "I'll call you. You're still at the Running H?"

"Yes. I'm not sure Ma — Mrs. Hoff will let me move into the log home, even if it is mine!" Patti confided.

"She's a fine person. So is her husband. They're my clients." The lawyer stowed the signed documents in his briefcase and smartly snapped it shut. "I trust this takes care of everything except the actual turning over of keys, bank books, etc. If you think of anything else, please drop by or call."

The finality in his tone made Patti feel he had washed his hands of her and was ready to move on to new business. She told him good-bye, tucked her precious letter in her purse, and walked out into a perfect autumn afternoon.

When she slid behind the wheel of the ranch station wagon the Hoffs had graciously lent her, Patti hesitated. "I'm not ready to go back to the Running H, Lord." She started the motor and pulled into the street. "I think I'll visit Dan's cabin. Mine, actually."

A curious thing happened to her while she drove. The numbness and disbelief she'd felt in the lawyer's office dissolved in the clear air. Wonderment came, along with gladness and humility. As much as she loved nursing, Patti had found herself dreading the need to return to work after the holidays. Now the need no longer existed. Dan had bequeathed the means to support herself and follow her dream of drawing and paint-

146

ing. *Why not use it to the utmost?*

Joy shot through her. Shepherd of Love had put no time limit on her leave of absence. Why not push aside all thoughts of when she would return? Or if? Patti couldn't imagine a better place anywhere to pursue her second dream. Surely she could find an art teacher in Kalispell. If not, she would purchase books on technique and diligently study them. The blazing fall countryside offered unlimited inspiration. Her new log home provided the solitude and peace needed to set her own schedule.

She reached the cabin and turned into the gravel driveway. Patti killed the engine and simply sat. Before her lay the scene she had painted from memory. Her golden leaves adorned the cottonwoods and formed great heaps at their bases.

She bowed her head in thankfulness and humility. "So much for one person," she murmured. "Lord, help me be worthy of Dan's trust in me. And Yours."

Patti stepped from the station wagon and walked around her newly acquired property. She ached for the thrilling moment she would unlock the front door and take possession of the place that held so many happy memories. Scuffing through the downed leaves, she decided she wouldn't change a thing, at least for now. Patti tilted her head back and gazed at the slowly swaying cottonwoods. *No wonder Dan Davis feared having the property fall into uncaring hands! Cutting such magnificent trees would be nothing short of sinful.*

Patti stayed until the sun rested on a western hill like a balancing rock, then reluctantly started back to the Running H. Dan and the Hoffs had warned her many times about miscalculating daylight. After the Montana sun set, night quickly followed, especially this time of year. Once away from the lights of Kalispell, no glow such as from lights of Seattle guided a traveler's way. Besides, the Hoffs would grow anxious if the nurse they had unofficially adopted as another daughter lingered away from the ranch after dark.

Patti sang all the way home sheltering hymns, such as "Rock of Ages" and "God Is My Strong Salvation." How far away trouble seemed! The last words of a song died on her lips. Charles Bradley had warned he never gave up what was his. Suppose he came to Montana?

Patti's hands tightened on the wheel. "If he learns of my inheritance, he's bound to show up," she grimly said. Strange how accurately she read the handsome pilot since the betraying glimpse into his real personality. "Well, he won't learn it from me, and I hope no one else tells him."

"So much for anonymity," she complained to the Hoffs a few days later. An enterprising reporter had unearthed news of Dan Davis's will. His story was splashed all over the front page of a leading Montana paper under the caption:

WELL KNOWN COWBOY/RANCHER
LEAVES BULK OF ESTATE TO SEATTLE
NURSE.

A basically accurate account followed, complete with photographs of Dan Davis and the Running H. It closed by saying the value of the estate was considerable but the exact amount unknown.

A few hours later, the Running H swarmed with TV camera crews and a flock of reporters.

"Better talk with them, Honey," Ma Hoff advised. "Just be careful."

Patti took the wise advice. She fended off personal questions and simply said, "Yes, I cared for Mr. Davis and drove him home at his request. He and the Hoffs gave me a wonderful vacation. His will surprised me, but I am grateful. I plan to stay in Kalispell

for a time. Beyond that, I have no plans."
She insisted the Hoffs pose with her when
the camera crew wanted more pictures. Ma
and Pa proved equally discreet and adept at
saying little or nothing.

"If they had simply stuck to the interview,
it wouldn't be so bad," Patti complained
when she and the Hoffs watched the evening
newscast. "It's bad enough being called an
angel of mercy and kindness. The speculation that I'm a schemer who took advantage
of Dan is worse."

"Folks who know you also know better,"
Ma reminded. "I wouldn't worry about the
others too much. Remember, even Jesus was
known for good and bad."

I wonder what Scott Sloan will believe. Patti
blushed. *Who cares? You do,* a little voice
accused. *Seeing doubt or contempt in his dark
eyes would hurt.* She squelched the idea,
then forgot it when the phone rang for her.

"Congratulations on your good fortune,"
Charles Bradley drawled. "No wonder you
were so eager to leave the bright lights of
Seattle and bury yourself in a Montana cow
town."

CHAPTER 9

"Hello, Sloan."

Scott stopped halfway between his Bell Jet-Ranger and Mike Parker's Rescue Service hangar and spun around. A ghost from his past stood waiting.

"What are you doing here?"

That same sardonic smile flashed on the intruder's handsome, mocking face. It had always filled Scott with an uncontrollable urge to wipe it off. "What kind of welcome is that from your old flight buddy?"

Scott clenched his fists and took a warning step forward.

Charles Bradley raised an eyebrow and fell back. "I actually came to see my fiancée. Just thought I'd drop by and renew an old acquaintance."

"Fiancée?" Scott felt like a trained parrot.

"Patti Thompson. The nurse who wormed her way into old man Davis's affections and inherited half of Kalispell." Triumph flamed in Charles's blue eyes. "It's easy street for yours truly from now on." His fists shot up. "Yes!"

The Rescue Service pilot felt like he'd been kicked in the stomach. He had written Patti Thompson off just as Bradley described her. Yet hearing her treachery fall from this man's lips sickened him. *He could be lying,* Scott reasoned. The gate to his heart he had slammed shut creaked, then clanged back into a locked position. *Charles could be right. Renewing an old acquaintance?* Scott sneered. If he never saw Charles Bradley again, it would be too soon. What cruel fate had sent first Patti Thompson, then Charles Bradley back into his life?

"I fail to see that anything in your life concerns me."

Some of the tension went out of the blond pilot's face.

"It concerns you. I understand your boss wants Patti as a rescue flight nurse. I won't have it."

"Don't cry on my shoulder. I'm no more excited about the idea than you are." Scott regretted the words the second they came out, especially when an avid expression came over Charles's face. It galled him to ask, and he hated the conciliatory tone in his voice, but added, "Don't go shouting it to Nurse Thompson. Flying with an enemy can be dangerous, as you already know."

Charles turned a furious red at the hidden meaning. He started to speak, then fixed his gaze over Scott's left shoulder and drawled in an unnecessarily loud voice, "So you're not excited about flying with my fiancée. Interesting."

"Very. And I'm not your fiancée, Charles." Icicles hung on the words.

Scott whirled. Mike Parker and Patti Thompson stood not ten feet away. She looked downright fetching in a trim denim jeans and jacket outfit with a red turtleneck and a matching bandanna at her throat. The nurse shot an annihilating gaze toward Charles before turning to Scott. He felt shriveled by the scorching look in her blue eyes.

"Mr. Parker wants you to show me your helicopter," she told him in a level voice.

The dark-haired pilot couldn't have moved if his life depended on it. No such paralysis attacked Bradley.

"That won't be necessary." He stepped forward and draped a possessive arm over Patti's shoulders. "Sorry, Parker. She isn't going to fly for you. Especially with Sloan."

Red flags waved in Mike's round face.

"I say she is. She says she is. What you or

anyone else thinks doesn't count." He leveled a glance at Scott.

Charles's face turned ugly. His fingers tightened. "Oh, yeah?"

"Yeah," Mike belligerently told him. "Now let her go and get off my property before I throw you off."

"You and who else?" Charles blustered.

"Better do what he says," Scott advised in a deadly voice.

"I suppose you're going to make me, the way you thought you'd make me —"

"Shut up and get going!" Mike bellowed. "If you come around again, I'll call the police and have you arrested for trespassing and causing trouble."

Patti jerked free from Charles's grasp and rubbed her shoulders. Scott saw her wince.

"That goes for me, too," she snapped.

Shock and a look akin to fear chased the smirk from Charles's face. "You can't mean that! What kind of lies have these guys cooked up? Don't let them turn you against me, Patti. I don't know what Parker's up to, but I know plenty about Sloan. More than any other man alive. I was there."

Pain shot through every part of Scott's body. All that kept his hands off the taunting man was the knowledge that if he once touched Charles, he might kill him. So much for all the years of trying to forgive his one enemy, to follow in Christ's foot-steps and rise above hatred and the desire for revenge. Cold sweat sprang to his fore-head. Scott pressed his arms close to his rigid body. In a few short minutes, the hard-won peace he'd felt gradually returning had deserted him.

Patti raised her chin and stared straight into Charles's face.

"Whatever is between you and Scott Sloan is your business. Your insisting I'm your fi-ancée is a lie. I told you we were through before I left Seattle. I also had no idea until after I came back to the Running H that Mr. Davis planned to leave me anything," she passionately went on. Scorn lashed like a quirt, leaving dull red streaks marring Charles's good looks. "I suspected you'd come running as soon as you learned about my inheritance. It didn't take you long to get here, did it?"

Scott wanted to shout "Bravo!" He wisely kept still, but began to revise his estimate of Patti. Her statements rang with truth. Maybe she hadn't known. Scott hid a smile. One thing for certain. Any love she may have felt for his old enemy no longer existed. Relief flowed through him, even while he mentally kicked himself for caring.

Charles groped for his obviously shaken self-confidence.

"I'm sorry, Darling." He turned on the charm Scott had seen create havoc so many times. "I can explain everything." He shot a glance of pure venom at Scott and Mike. "Just five minutes away from these louts, Patti," he wheedled. "You owe me that."

Sticks and stones will break my bones, but names and faces won't hurt me. The old nursery answer to challenges sang through Scott's mind and made him feel better. He grinned at Mike Parker, who loftily observed, "Sloan and I've been called a lot worse things than louts by a lot better persons than you, Bradley. Now make tracks, with the heel toward my hangar."

A ripple of mirth at Mike's sally escaped Patti's tightly closed lips. It grew into full-scale hilarity.

"I owe you nothing," she said when she stopped laughing.

Naked hatred sprang into Charles's eyes. Scott took an involuntary step toward the girl, fearing the rage he knew lurked inside the unwelcome visitor. Even all those years ago, Bradley never stood for anyone laughing at him. Now he clenched and unclenched his hands then turned his fury from Patti to Scott.

156

"Don't think this is over. You came between me and what I wanted once before, remember? I beat you then and I'll beat you now. My fiancée is suffering from overwork, on the verge of a nervous breakdown. I suggest you get her full medical reports before taking her on a mercy flight. Another accident would be inconvenient, to say the least."

God, help me let him walk away, Scott fervently prayed. Strength he hadn't believed possible came. Charles marched off after his cryptic threat like a soldier who loses a minor skirmish but knows the final victory is already his.

"Unpleasant cuss," Mike Parker announced. "Scott, if you'll show Patti the chopper, I'll get back to my paperwork." He hesitated. "Uh, you both might want to watch your step. Our departed guest reminds me of a rattlesnake, even down to rattling off a warning."

"Sorry you had to be let in for that," Scott said with regret when they walked to the waiting Bell Jet-Ranger.

"So am I." Her clipped tones showed she hadn't forgiven his comment about not wanting her to fly with him. All traces of former friendliness had vanished.

Scott felt he had lost something precious.

"I only kept my hands off Bradley by the grace of God."

"I can fight my own battles. Now, about the helicopter?"

Scott had the sensation of being inexorably frozen. "One more thing. Don't underestimate Charles Bradley. He never gives up anything he considers his."

Patti's slim shoulders dropped. She suddenly looked small and vulnerable.

"Thanks for the warning, but he already told me that." A wobbly smile brought a rush of admiration for her valor. "By the way, I *am* capable of flying or I never would have consented. Being here has done wonders for me. A recent checkup proved it." Her defiant gaze met his. "One other thing. If you're still reluctant to fly with me after our first mission, I'll ask Mike to use me elsewhere."

"If you handle that mission as well as you handled Bradley, I'll have no objection to working with you," he told her. "Truce?" Scott held out his hand.

Patti looked surprised. Her lips twitched and she shook with him. "Truce."

By the time Scott finished his first teaching session, Patti knew more about helicopters than she ever dreamed she'd need to learn. The white Bell Jet-Ranger, with its red cross and trim, fully lived up to and beyond Pa Hoff's description of it as a flying First Aid station. Manned by an expert pilot and trained medical help, Patti realized it would be a godsend to those in isolated areas.

This particular model chopper had two front seats, for pilot and nurse or doctor, plus a rear bench that would hold three passengers. Standard equipment included a two-person survival pack. Patti marveled. *So much necessary material stowed in the orange backpack that weighed only six pounds and measured eleven inches wide, ten inches high, and four inches deep!*

"Everything to stay alive, including MRE: meal, ready to eat," Scott translated. He gave Patti a list of contents to study. "This will help you know how to pack your medical bag," he soberly told her. "We don't break into the survival pack unless it's an emergency."

She carefully tucked the list into her jacket pocket. A quiver went through her. "Have you ever needed one?"

"Yes." To her disappointment, Scott didn't elaborate.

"I have so much to learn," Patti admitted when he finished explaining the hazards of the job.

She felt his keen gaze on her before he suggested, "Would you like to go up today for a dry run? I don't want to discourage you, Nurse Thompson, but some people can't stand riding in a chopper. It's a lot different than flying fixed-wing. I've hauled a lot of folks who get sick, no matter how often they fly with me."

"My goodness, I never thought of that!" Patti gasped. "I hope I'm not one of them. By the way, Nurse Thompson sounds awfully formal if we're going to work together."

"Okay, Patti. How about a ride?"

She glanced at her jeans outfit. "Is this okay for flying?"

"Put the bandanna over your hair and it will be perfect. Of course, this winter you'll want a sheepskin coat, fleece-lined boots, insulated gloves, that kind of thing." He grinned at her and Patti felt her heart lift. Disapproval from others always depressed her. "That is, if you survive today's flight."

"All right." She trotted along beside him, to keep up with his long stride.

Shoulder harness in place, Scott turned his full attention to her.

"For your own protection, I need to put the chopper through its full paces," he quietly said. "This isn't to scare you or a ploy to make you quit before starting. It's imperative for you to learn whether your system can take sudden drops caused by down drafts, that kind of thing."

Her heart flew to her throat and parked there. "I understand. Do your best. I mean your worst. Oh, dear, I'm babbling."

Scott's clear laugh rang out, a contagious sound that restored her to normal.

Too bad he didn't use it more often. It changed him from Stone Face to a living, breathing human being.

The thrill of Patti's first helicopter ride made a lasting impression. Despite Scott's warning, she hadn't realized how very different helicopter flights were from regular airplanes, or "fixed wing" as Scott called them. Here there was no taxiing down a runway, just a thrust up from the tarmac then flying thousands of feet lower than in commercial planes, feeling she could reach down and touch the tops of trees. Such maneuverability she wasn't prepared for even from watching popular TV shows that featured helicopters.

Patti knew her face glowed when they returned and landed.

"I love it!" she squealed, forgetting the man beside her hadn't really wanted her to fly with him. She clambered out of the chopper, knocking off her red scarf. Patti ran to a broadly grinning Mike Parker, who had deserted his paperwork and come out to meet the returning travelers.

"Well, how did she do?" He sounded impatient.

Scott dangled the bandanna from one hand. "She passed with flying colors." He waved the scarf back and forth like a banner.

Patti wanted to hug him. Instead, she grabbed the bandanna and did a little jig. "When can I go on a real mission? Soon, I hope." She felt herself redden. "I don't mean I want anyone to get sick or hurt. I'm just excited about flying."

"In the meantime, you may want to review everything you know about making do and nursing under primitive conditions," Mike suggested.

Patti touched her jacket pocket. "Yes, and I'll study the list of what's in the survival pack as if my life depends on it."

Scott frowned at her comment. "Do that. Sometime it may." He walked away before she could tell him she was serious, not being facetious.

"Oh dear, now he's upset with me again," Patti mourned.

Mike awkwardly patted her shoulder. "Don't worry about Stone Face. He carries heavier burdens than most men. Glad you'll be working with us." He walked her to the Bronco and courteously waited until she drove away.

That night, Patti settled down in the living room of her inherited log cabin. A fire crackled in the fireplace and cast rosy shadows on the off-white walls. The plushy dark green carpet stretched beneath her slippered feet like a forest floor. How she loved it all! Here she had found rest. Here the turmoil of many weeks and months seemed long ago and mercifully far away — until today.

Patti shifted position and grimaced. A twinge of pain reminded her of Charles's fingers biting into her shoulder. She thought of the faint blue marks she'd seen after she showered and slipped into a warm fleece robe. Again she gave thanks. Prayer gave way to speculation. *What shared experience had created the animosity between Scott Sloan and Charles Bradley?* she wondered.

"Something shattering enough to turn them into lifetime enemies," she murmured. Snatches of Charles's bitter accusations returned.

"I suppose you're going to make me, the way you thought you'd make me —"

"I know plenty about Sloan. More than

163

any other man alive. I was there."

"You came between me and what I wanted once before, remember? I beat you then and I'll beat you now."

"Another accident would be inconvenient, to say the least."

"Worse than trying to put a jigsaw puzzle together," Patti decided aloud. One more conversation fragment returned. Both Scott Sloan's face and voice had definitely warned when he remarked, "One more thing. Don't underestimate Charles Bradley. He never gives up anything he considers his."

Patti shook off the apprehension the warning brought. What could Charles do but accept her ultimatum? And Mike Parker's, to keep away from the Rescue Service property? Why did the home in which she had felt so secure suddenly feel just a little too isolated?

"Lord, now that I have my own place, maybe I should get a dog." The idea grew more appealing with every moment. On impulse, she called the Hoffs.

When Ma answered, Patti breathlessly asked, "Where would a person go if he, in this case she, decided to get a dog? Besides in a pound, I mean. They don't always have the kind you want."

"Where you get a good dog depends on if

you want a real dog, a rag mop, or a rat," Ma promptly told her. She laughed. "In other words, what breed?"

"One that will bark if anyone comes around, but won't make the closest neighbors wish I'd never moved in," Patti replied.

Ma's voice sharpened. "Is there something you aren't telling me?"

"Charles Bradley showed up today. He claimed me as his fiancée in front of Scott Sloan and Mike Parker. I told him off. Mike told him off. Scott and Charles threw a few verbal bombs and my ex — as in highly ex-fiancé — intimated I was on the verge of a nervous breakdown and unfit to fly. Mike ordered him to leave and not come back," Patti summed up.

"Is that all?" Ma sounded relieved. "I thought it might be something serious."

Patti had to cover the mouthpiece to keep from howling into her friend's ear.

"I'd say that was quite enough! By the way, Scott took me up in the helicopter and checked me out. I have a job. I mean, I'm officially cleared to fly."

"Good." Ma never wasted much time on unnecessary talk, especially on the telephone. "About the dog. I'll ask around and see if anyone has one they can't keep and that needs a good home. A Labrador would be good. They aren't mean like some dogs, but their bark will scare the sheet off a ghost!"

The excited nurse hung up, still laughing. *Leave it to Ma Hoff.* The capable woman would probably find the exact dog to best meet Patti's needs and deliver it to the log cabin before its new owner could lay in a supply of dog food!

Patti washed a juicy apple in the kitchen and brought it back to her seat in front of the fire. Now to study the list of survival pack contents. She found it arranged in six basic groups necessary for survival and rescue. She read aloud, "Medical and First Aid Group. First Aid and burn cream. Small and large butterfly closures. Gauze roll and surgical tape. Sheer strips, gauze pads, and elastic bandage. Wound compressors. Complete snake-bite kit. Cotton pellets and pain-relief drops. Metal tweezers, toothache kit, antiseptic towelettes. Ammonia inhalants, throat lozenges, and aspirin tablets. Salt tablets. Antihistamine, antacid, and anti-diarrhea tablets.

"Goodness, it really is complete," Patti exclaimed. "Let's see what's under the Food and Water group. Water/fuel storage container, canteens, tropical chocolate bar, water-purification tablets, tea bags, fruit drink packs, sugar bags, soup packs, granola bars, and chewing gum." She nodded approval.

"Signal and Light Group. Cyalume light sticks? I can ask Scott what they are. Whistle, aerial flares, orange smoke signal, signal flag, long burn candle, signal mirror. Emergency Devices Group. Utility knife, nylon rope, copper wire. Razor blade, safety pins, liquid-filled compass, toilet tissue, and survival manual."

More impressed with every item, Patti continued. "Shelter and Protection Group. Large, orange, two-person tent. Emergency space blankets. Sunglasses, insect repellent, and sunburn protection. Fire and Cooking Group. Waterproof matches, two fuel bars, one-quart metal pot, two pint containers."

She laid aside the list, heart pumping. "God forbid we ever need all this stuff, but I'm so thankful it will be on hand."

Patti rose and crossed to the window. She pulled aside the drapes enough to notice a high-riding, tipsy-looking moon. Suppose the worst happened? What if she and Scott Sloan were pitted against the wilderness of western Montana?

A glow that had nothing to do with the fire warming her hearth stole into her cheeks. How ironic that of all the men Patti

167

had ever known, Stone Face would be her first choice as a companion with whom to be stranded in the wilds.

Would she be his?

"Don't be absurd," Patti said. "He doesn't even like me."

So change his mind, a little voice advised. *Scott Sloan is well worth knowing.*

Patti restlessly reached for sketchpad and pencil. A rough image of the pilot emerged. Disgusted with herself for acting like a lovestruck adolescent, she crumpled the page and threw it in the fire. It would take more chipping away than she felt capable of doing to make a dent in Stone Face's reserve.

CHAPTER 10

Two major events occurred in Patti Thompson's life almost simultaneously.

First, she acquired a housebroken, guaranteed-not-to-chew-the-furniture, half-grown black Labrador named Obsidian.

"What a strange name!" she commented to the Hoffs, who had taken her to a distant ranch to get acquainted with the dog. "Isn't that the natural glass made when hot lava cools quickly?"

"Obsidian is black. So is the dog." Pa Hoff's matter-of-fact explanation made Patti want to giggle. He obviously saw nothing odd about the name.

"Indians used obsidian to make arrowheads. Have you ever been to Yellowstone Park?" Ma put in.

"No, but I would like to go. Maybe next spring." Patti gave a happy little bounce.

"Take a look at Obsidian Cliff, an enormous mass of obsidian worth seeing."

Patti admitted the name fit when she saw the black Labrador lying on the ranch house porch beside his master's chair.

"You darling!" She plumped to her knees and held out one hand. Pa had primed her on how to approach a dog on their ride to the ranch. Obsidian needed to accept her before she took him home.

The dog's clear brown eyes looked trustingly into hers. He sniffed, licked her hand, and cocked his head.

"He's trying to decide about me," Patti said. "I hope I pass the test!"

She told the dog, "We're going to be friends, Obsidian."

He nosed her hand, crept closer, and pressed his well-shaped head against her jeans. Patti laid her hand on his head and stroked. A quick wriggle brought him even closer. She put both arms around his silky body and hugged him. Obsidian rewarded her with a face-washing and a bark that started from his toes. It really would scare the sheet off a ghost!

"May I take him with me?" Patti asked the rancher who owned him.

"No reason why not. He's sure taken to you," the weather-beaten man cleared his throat. "I hate to see him go, but my wife isn't well. In fact, she's already in Helena with our son. We've sold out so we can be closer to him. A city's no fit place for a big dog. He needs to roam. Same goes for his owner, but things don't always stay the way a man wants." His keen gaze bore into Patti. "I hear Dan Davis left you his log cabin. You'll have plenty of room for Obsidian there. He's an outdoor dog, so I'll send along his dog house. He's used to it, so don't be bringing him inside, especially to sleep, unless something scares you." He paused before saying, "My wife and I took Obsidian with us a few times when we dropped in on Dan. It won't be like he's going somewhere totally strange."

"Will he run away when I'm gone?" Patti asked, petting the sleek head.

"I've heard of dogs that go back to their original owners' homes."

Pa Hoff spoke up. "Naw. The boys and I'll put up a fence this afternoon quicker than you can say scat."

"You won't have to cut down the cotton-woods, will you?" Patti worried. Her voice trembled. "One reason Dan left me his home was because he knew I loved it the way it was. He said if I ever decided to sell it, to make sure it wasn't to someone who's likely to rip out the cottonwoods."

She started to add Dan had also suggested

she offer the home first to Scott Sloan. A sharp thrust of suspicion stopped her. *Was that the reason for the distrust in Stone Face's eyes? Had he hoped Dan would leave the log cabin to him?* Learning someone else had inherited the place he loved was bound to leave a sour taste in Scott's mouth. Especially when that someone was a nurse Dan Davis had never heard of until a few months before he changed his will.

"Miss?"

Patti jerked herself back to the present. "Yes?"

"Are you planning to sell? It could make a difference about Obsidian. I'd hate for him to just get settled and have you head off to Seattle," he told her bluntly.

She stared at the concerned rancher. Perhaps he was right. After a long, soul-searching moment she told him, "I have no plans to leave Kalispell. I love my new home and look forward to flying for Mike Parker." Patti drew in a long breath and slowly expelled it. "On the other hand, I can't promise to stay in Montana forever. I can promise one thing. If I ever leave, I'll take as much care in finding a good home for Obsidian as you are doing now."

"Shucks," Ma Hoff put in. "If Patti ever flies the coop, we'll take care of your dog.

Same goes if she gets caught out overnight on a rescue flight. No trouble at all for one of us or a hand of ours to drive in and make sure he's okay."

The rancher visibly relaxed. "Good enough for me." He shook Patti's hand. She felt calluses born of hard work press into her palm. "I'd kinda like to say good-bye to Obsidian by my lonesome." He smiled at Patti. "My wife said on the phone that anyone Dan Davis trusted with his possessions would take good care of our dog." He snapped his fingers. The dog leaped from Patti's arms and followed the rancher off the porch and toward the Hoffs' station wagon.

"His heart's broken at having to leave this place," Ma Hoff observed.

Patti nodded, too filled with emotion to speak. She glanced at the rancher and his dog. Obsidian stood rigid as the Yellowstone cliff with the same name. A few minutes later, man and dog returned. Sadness lurked in the rancher's eyes, but he smiled and placed Patti's hand on Obsidian's back.

"Go with her, Boy." He walked onto the porch and into the house without looking back.

Obsidian stayed, but gazed after his owner. The puzzled expression in his eyes when he turned back to Patti nearly broke her heart. Again she knelt and put her arms around him.

"It's okay, Obsidian. He will be all right. So will you." She stood, one hand on his head. "Shouldn't we, I mean, don't I owe for the dog?"

"It would be an insult to offer him money," Pa Hoff quietly told her.

Patti flushed at her insensitivity. "Of course it would. Come, Obsidian." He followed her into the back seat of the station wagon, pressed his nose to the window, and watched until a bend of the road hid the ranch house. Then he sighed, lay down, and put his head on Patti's knee.

When they arrived at the log cabin, Obsidian perked up. He trotted around the property, sniffing and occasionally barking. Patti let him explore, but he looked so forlorn sitting on her porch, she didn't have the heart to leave him there alone. All afternoon she ran and played with him to the tune of pounding and men's voices. Before nightfall, a hastily constructed but serviceable fence enclosed her property. Obsidian's dog house settled beneath a large cottonwood as if it had been there since the land began.

"Thank you so much," she told the workers.

They doffed sombreros, Stetsons, and straw hats according to individual taste and grinned.

"A pleasure to be neighborly," one said.

Another, bolder than the rest, added, "It 'pears you're aimin' to stay a spell, what with gettin' a dawg and buildin' a fence, and all."

He sounded so much like Dan Davis, Patti had to blink back tears. "I am."

" 'Course she is," Pa Hoff defended. "That's why Dan left her this place." He pounded a final nail and laughed. "C'mon, boys. We're through here and it's almost supper time. Cookie means it when he yells 'come and git it or I'll throw it out the window.' "

The hands scrambled into the station wagon and a couple of other vehicles. A chorus of good-byes brought an answering bark from Obsidian. Patti waved until they were out of sight, then started inside. The dog's nails clicked on the porch floor behind her, but he made no attempt to follow her into the house. She fought against the desire to let him sleep inside for at least the first night and won. It simply meant postponing the inevitable. Tomorrow night wouldn't be any easier for Obsidian — or her.

Patti opened a can of dog food and broke

it apart in one of the bowls she had purchased for her new pet's exclusive use. She poured fresh water into the second, praying Obsidian would eat. The Hoffs had warned he might take a few days to adjust. "Don't force him," they warned. "Let him decide."

To Patti's joy, he ate every morsel and licked the bowl. He lapped water and sat down on the doormat when she went back into the house. Twice before getting ready for bed, she went out and petted the dog. At last, she turned off the living room lights except for those on automatic timer and went to her bedroom. She heard the familiar scrabble of Obsidian's nails on the porch and glanced out the front window of her bedroom.

Her dog stood just outside looking in with intelligent eyes. Patti opened the window and said through the screen, "It's okay, Boy." A bright idea came. She left the window, ran to a closet, and unearthed the oldest of the blankets Dan Davis had left behind. She took it outside and spread it beneath her window. "Here's a bed for you, if you like it better than your dog house," she told Obsidian. "Lie down and try it out."

The dog turned in a circle, then settled on the blanket and licked her hand. Patti suspected the spot would become his permanent bed until cold weather forced him to seek better shelter. Icy winter winds would surely blow across the roofed, open-sided porch.

"I won't ask the Hoffs for any more favors," she told the dog. "But I think I'll inquire about carpenters. It wouldn't take much to enclose the porch. Just the ends. I won't do anything to shut out my view of the sunsets." She gave Obsidian a final pat and headed to bed. It had been a long and exciting day. Her last thought was of the dog on guard. No one could approach her window or the front of the house without disturbing her new barking machine. Patti fell asleep smiling at the ridiculous description.

The shrilling telephone tore Patti away from sketching late mid-morning of the next day.

"We need you," Mike Parker stated flatly. "Sloan's been notified. My other nurses are scheduled or down with the creeping awfuls."

Patti wondered what on earth the "creeping awfuls" were but bit back the remark that none of her medical texts described such a malady.

"Be there soon."

"Right." The call ended as abruptly as it began.

Thank goodness it wasn't too far from the log cabin to the flying field. Patti quickly dialed the Hoffs.

"On my way out," she said tersely. "Would you please call me this evening, just in case? If you get the answering machine, it means we had to stay overnight. I fed Obsidian this morning, but he is supposed to eat twice a day. The way he gobbled dinner last night, I'm afraid he will stuff himself and be miserable if I leave extra food out."

"Be glad to help. Happy flying, Honey."

Bless Ma Hoff. She conveyed more in a few words than many people did in hours of conversation! Patti scrambled into her jeans outfit, substituting a navy scarf and turtleneck for the red set. She slapped together a belated breakfast: a multi-grain peanut butter sandwich. She also gulped down a glass of orange juice and reminded herself to buy bananas. They made great quick-energy snacks. Halfway to the hangar, she let up on the gas pedal.

"Great! I forgot to ask Mike about a lunch. Am I supposed to keep one packed, just in case?" She shook her head and grinned at the gorgeous fall morning. "At least I won't starve. There are always the food supplies in the survival pack."

A short time later, Patti swung the red Bronco she loved driving into the parking lot next to the hangar. She locked it, stowed her keys in the medical bag she'd packed the day after getting approved for flight, and hurried into Mike Parker's office.

"Reporting for duty, Sir."

"It sure didn't take you long," Mike praised. His brows drew together in a frown. "I hope you had breakfast. Can't have you getting weak in the knees."

Patti nodded until her blond hair bounced beneath the navy bandanna tied gypsy-fashion. "Yes. Where are we going?"

Scott Sloan stepped through the door. "To bring in two hikers who shouldn't be allowed out of city limits." He shook his dark head. "They drove an ATV — that's an all-terrain vehicle — into the wilderness, parked it and started hiking. A few miles in, they tried to cross a steep gravel slope. Both fell. One thinks he may have fractured ribs. The other went back to the vehicle and sent out a call for help. A trucker picked it up and relayed it. I wish people would learn you don't tackle western Montana's mountains and canyons unless you're mighty sure of what you're doing. Even then, it's risky." A slight smile smoothed away his frown.

"Ready?"

"Uh-huh." She nodded again and followed him to the waiting Bell Jet-Ranger. Once inside, Patti buckled up as Scott had taught her. She felt again the exhilaration when they lifted off.

"How far do we have to go?" she asked.

"Less than a hundred miles. Roughly forty-five minutes flying time." Scott expertly headed the helicopter north and west.

Patti marveled at the scene below them. Shining silver rivers threaded the land. Foothills sloped upward and became part of the Rockies. Their snowy caps warned winter lay just ahead. It lurked in shadowy glens, dying leaves, heavily-mossed boulders. Scott flew low enough to point out animals. A herd of powerful elk stood poised, then sprang away from the buzz of the helicopter. A fat bear batted fish from a glistening stream.

"I wish I'd brought my sketch pad." Patti sighed. "Not that I can ever do this justice." Memory of the sketch she'd made of the man beside her sent fire to her cheeks. *Good thing Scott didn't know about it.*

"No one but God can ever really do justice to what we see on these flights," Scott said soberly. "Have you always wanted to draw?"

Patti told him the same story she had shared with Dan Davis months earlier.

"This winter I plan to take classes, or study. For the first time in my life, I'll have time. I will, won't I? I suppose flights slow down in winter?"

Scott shrugged. "It can go either way, depending on weather. We get called on to help Search and Rescue teams, the Ski Patrol, that kind of thing. There are also calls from people who get snowed in and can't make it to a doctor." He laughed. "We get all kinds of calls. Last year I flew a nurse in to answer a frantic call for a female in labor. Turned out it was a cow trying to deliver a calf breech!" He chuckled reminiscently.

Patti tensed. "What did you do?"

"Followed orders from the nurse and helped Mother Nature along. Cow, calf, nurse, and pilot all survived." He laughed again. "I'll never forget the look on the nurse's face when the rancher announced he was naming the calf Sarah. I thought she'd split. Good sport, though. She told the grateful owner to take good care of her 'namesake.' However, when we got back, the nurse glared and said, 'Not one word from either of you, or I'm through.'" Scott shot Patti an amused glance. "How would

181

you like to have a critter named after you?"

"I can't picture a calf called Patti," she demurely said. Thankfulness for the relaxed atmosphere between them sent a silent prayer upwards. Flying and working with an incompatible coworker would be miserable. She also gave thanks for Scott's outstanding flying skills. On reaching their destination, he hovered the chopper over a spot close to the two men frantically waving their arms. Patti swallowed hard and hid her shaking hands in her jacket pockets. *How could he land a helicopter on such a precarious-looking perch?*

Scott brought the chopper down. Blessed silence followed.

"Ready?"

"Ready." Patti grabbed her well-packed medical bag and stepped out to begin her first case. *What a far cry from Shepherd of Love, with all its modern equipment!* There was no array of sterilized instruments, no hum of muted voices as doctors and nurses reassured patients; only the mournful cry of a flock of wild geese getting a late start south gave an eerie mood to the scene. A mountain goat bleated down at them from a cliff above the narrow strip of level land where they'd set down. It made Patti wonder if she were really here, or dreaming.

A few questions brought the same story the trucker had relayed. Patti caught Scott's quick glance at the hikers' inadequate shoes. No wonder they had slipped and fallen.

"Better get the right kind of footgear before doing any more hiking in the mountains," he advised.

Patti forced her attention to her patients. A quick examination brought a sigh of relief. One hiker had suffered little more than abrasions and contusions. Scott administered first aid while Patti examined the second man.

"I wanted to walk out with my friend," he reported. "Couldn't make it. Climbing made me cough and brought excruciating pain." He winced when she touched his rib cage.

"You'll be fine, although you may have fractured a rib." Patti smiled, thankful he had no trouble breathing, a symptom of a punctured lung.

"What do you do for him?" the friend wanted to know. "Tape him?"

"Not anymore. It's best to simply get him to the hospital. They'll X-ray."

"Since I don't have much wrong with me, is it okay to drive out?"

Patti nodded and Scott said, "We'll take you back to your vehicle. You've probably had enough hiking for one day."

"Thanks." He looked embarrassed. "Uh, you're a private company, aren't you? What about charges?"

"You will receive a bill." Scott turned to the more badly injured hiker. "Ready?"

Patti heaved a sigh of relief after an uneventful flight back to Kalispell. Alerted by Scott, Mike had an ambulance waiting. Patti watched the medics load the accident victim and murmured, "Thus endeth the first flight. What next?"

"We report in. That is, you report, then Mike asks me if I have anything to add. I normally don't." He sent her an oblique, unreadable look.

Normally? Does that mean he has something to add today? Patti wondered. She tried to think. Had she done something wrong? Nothing came to mind.

"So how did it go?" Mike eagerly inquired when they entered the office.

Patti briefed him.

"Anything to add?" the flight service owner asked Scott, as usual.

Stone Face didn't move a muscle. "Yeah."

Mike's mouth dropped open. Patti's heart dropped to her toes like an out-of-control elevator going down. *Uh-oh. That sounds like trouble.*

Scott flipped off the baseball cap he wore while flying.

"I don't want Thompson flying with me when she's not up with the other pilots."

What happened to calling me Patti? she wondered. Then she inwardly blazed, *You—you jerk!* The words wouldn't come out.

Mike's round face turned purple. He leaped from his chair and glowered at his pilot.

"Flight assignments are my call, not yours."

"Let me finish, okay? I'm requesting her on a permanent basis, any time she's willing to fly."

Parker dropped back into his chair. "Of all the — what's with you, Stone Face?"

Scott crossed his arms behind his head. A twinkle began in his eyes and he counted on strong, lean fingers.

"One, she knows her business. Two, she knows when to talk and when to keep still. She comments on the scenery but doesn't gush. Three, there wasn't a peep out of her when I landed in a tricky spot. I could tell she was nervous, but she didn't let on."

"Anything else?" Mike barked.

Scott hesitated and looked uncertain.

"I'll tell you later," he mumbled.

Patti roused from the roller-coaster swing

she had ridden from the depths of anger to pride and amazement at the unexpected praise.

"Since it's obviously about me, I'd like to hear it," she said in a tight voice.

Was that an all-right-you-asked-for-it glint in Stone Face's watching eyes?

He raised an eyebrow, then turned and spoke to Mike as though Patti had remained at the rescue site.

"There's no place in my business for a flight nurse who calls attention to the fact she's a woman and I'm a man. Patti doesn't." He followed his succinct evaluation with a comradely grin.

Scarlet and tongue-tied, she watched him unhurriedly stride across the room and go out whistling.

"Well, I never!"

"Neither did I." Mike Parker agreed. A strange expression settled on his full moon face. "Never in all the time he's been flying for me has Stone Face requested one nurse over another. What did you do to him?"

Patti speechlessly shook her head. She wished she knew!

CHAPTER 11

Only one thing stood between Patti Thompson — homeowner and rescue flight nurse — and complete contentment: Charles Bradley, who kept popping up like a wicked jack-in-the box. Following his first dramatic reappearance in Patti's life, he began a "now you see me, now you don't" game that kept her on edge.

"How can he take so much time off from his job?" she asked Obsidian one sunny afternoon while romping with him in her fenced yard. "Charles raged when I planned to come here early. He said he had to pull strings to get off for the month of December. Now I can't turn around without seeing him. Is he banking on winning me back, along with my inheritance? Has he gone so far as to quit his job in hopes of wearing me down?"

Obsidian obligingly gave a sympathetic bark and ran after the tennis ball Patti pitched into the air. He leaped and caught it before it fell to the ground.

"At least Charles can't follow me when I'm out on a rescue mission," she rejoiced. "I suspect Stone Face would welcome an excuse to boot my persistent ex-fiancé out of the chopper."

Annoyance with Charles transferred to Scott. Although Patti seldom admitted it even to herself, she had hoped his requesting her to fly with him meant the beginning of real friendship. It hadn't. At times she felt tempted to use feminine wiles and crash through the invisible barrier her coworker kept firmly in place. Each time she violently rejected the idea. The one thing Stone Face definitively admired about her was her lack of flirting. Why risk his contempt by showing she admired far more about him than his flying skills?

"He only wants a buddy, not a sweetheart," Patti admitted. "Now where did that gem of rhetoric come from?" She scanned her memory. "Oh, yes. Grandma Thompson used to sing a song with words that made a lot of sense." If Patti remembered correctly, it had been handed down from her great-grandmother and World War I times. "What's the rest of it?" she asked Obsidian.

His ears perked up and he brought her

the ball to throw again.

Patti laughed. "Some help you are!" She hummed the tune. Words came back. She sang them, wondering if the writer had based the song on a sad experience.

I only want a buddy, not a sweetheart.
    Buddies never make you blue. Sweet-
    hearts make vows that are broken,
    broken like my heart is broken, too.
Don't tell me that you love me, say you
    like me,
No lover's quarrels, no honeymoon for two.
Don't turn down lover's lane, but keep on
    just the same,
I only want a buddy, not a gal.

A hateful laugh followed the final note of her song. Patti turned toward the man lounging against her new fence.

"What are you doing here?"

"Watching you and our honeymoon cabin. Not a bad place."

A crimson tide washed into Patti's face. Charles's appraising look at the house and herself made her feel she'd been put on the auction block, to be sold to the highest bidder.

"Go away or I'm calling the police." The anger in her voice must have rung a warning bell in Obsidian's alert brain. He barked and raced toward the fence.

Patti followed. She'd never seen the black lab in action as a guard dog. She doubted he would clear the fence and take a chunk out of Charles, but didn't dare chance it.

"Down, Boy!" she called sharply. "Sit, Obsidian!"

The barking broke off mid-howl. The dog hesitated, then obeyed.

Charles sprang back from the fence, face contorted with rage.

"Better chain that mutt before he attacks someone who will sue you," he snarled.

"Don't get any ideas," Patti flung back at him. "Obsidian is on his property, protecting it — and me." Her steady gaze met Charles's and she added significantly, "He also sleeps just below my window, in case trespassers or unwanted visitors pay a night call. Now, are you going, or must I call the authorities and get a restraining order to keep you away from here?"

"Fat chance." Charles smirked. "You have no grounds. The police would laugh at you." He abruptly changed tactics. "Forgive me, Patti. My world fell apart when you walked out on me." He took a deep breath and looked from her to the log home. "Seeing all this and remembering how we planned to spend our honeymoon here is harder than you'll ever know." Misery clouded his eyes.

"That song also brings back memories. If you won't be my sweetheart, please, at least be my friend. I'm too weak to be the kind of person I know I should be. With you, I can make it. I haven't been worthy, yelling at you and everything, but I pray every day you'll give me another chance. My whole life's at stake."

Caught off guard by Charles's apparent sincerity, Patti felt herself weakening. He evidently saw it. Excitement over his impending victory flashed across his face and he overplayed his pretense of humility.

"I knew you couldn't turn me down," he exulted. "You're a Christian. That means you have to forgive me."

Patti stared at the man she had so nearly married. Fear replaced pity and she shivered. The man before her definitely showed classic symptoms of mental illness, berating her one moment, pleading with her the next.

Charles put a hand on the gate. Confidence shone in the jaunty step he took forward.

"Call off your dog, will you, Darling?"

Obsidian's warning growl loosened Patti's frozen tongue.

191

"If you want my forgiveness, you have it," she said. "I'm afraid anything else just isn't possible. Find a woman who really loves you, Charles. Someone you can be true to for the rest of your life." She took a deep breath. "I'm sorry, but it won't be me."

"It's Sloan, isn't it? Do you know you're in love with a murderer? He was cleared at a hearing, but it doesn't change the fact he was guilty as sin."

Why must blood rush to her face making her appear even more guilty? Patti furiously wondered. "You don't — you can't mean Stone Face!"

"So that's what they call him now. The families of the two persons he killed had other names for him." Charles laughed unpleasantly. "Chain the dog and I'll tell you a bedtime story that will curl your hair tighter than it is now. I've kept track of Sloan for years. I knew he was here. That's why I objected when you planned to come here without me to protect you. It was for your own good."

Patti's world spun like a Ferris wheel before her training on how to handle critical situations kicked in. A barrage of mental images of Scott Sloan came to her rescue. *Murderer? Never in a million years! Yet*

Charles Bradley's statements held the ring of truth.

That's it, Patti decided. *Not truth, but clever deceit that fooled me before.* The thought steadied her.

Charles ignored her silence and continued his harangue. "He tried to make me lie. Said I was the only one who could clear him. Even if it had been true, I wouldn't have done it. He came between me and a girl I tried to protect from nasty gossip. That's why he hates me." His lips curled back. "I hear he's posing as a Christian now, pillar of the community and all that. If the hearing board had listened to me the way they should have, Sloan would be in jail."

"He said you could clear him?" Suspicion popped into Patti's mind like crocuses through snow. She didn't dare add the question that burned in her soul: *Was Scott really responsible, or were you?*

"I told you I was there." His eyes turned mocking. "Sorry. If you want the rest of the story, as Paul Harvey says, you have to let me in."

With suspicion came freedom and the courage to say, "If I want the rest of the story, I'll ask Scott Sloan."

Patti wasn't prepared for the violent reaction that followed. Charles tensed. For a moment she thought he would burst through the gate and attack her.

"On guard, Obsidian!" she cried.

The black lab leaped toward the fence. Charles backed away.

"You win, this time. Just remember, your dog won't always be with you." He walked down the gravel drive and started up the road.

The fact Charles had taken the precaution to park some distance away from her home turned Patti's knees to quivering gelatin. Once before she had been in terrible danger because of misjudging a man. This time, she would be prepared. She ran into the house and dialed the police.

Charles had been wrong when he warned her the authorities would laugh. The officers who responded found nothing funny in the situation. Patti told them exactly what happened, only omitting the part about Scott. She felt guilty, but couldn't bring herself to reopen old wounds until after she talked with the sober-faced pilot. The fierce desire to protect him raised questions in her mind, ones she must face and answer later. Reporting Charles's threat must come first.

"Do you know where this Bradley is staying?" the female officer asked.

"No. I assume his employer, possibly

194

former employer now, would."

"I want you to seriously consider this before answering, Miss Thompson. As a nurse who has dealt with unstable patients, has Charles Bradley's rage, his level of violence, escalated since the first time you saw that side of him?"

"Definitely."

The officers exchanged meaningful looks. "We'll be in touch," the policewoman said. "In the meantime, don't fall for any phony attempts that can result in making you vulnerable. Let's face it. Bradley sounds unscrupulous. You're an attractive woman. You're also desirable because of your inheritance."

She looked regretful. "I'm not trying to terrify you. Just be careful."

"What kind of thing do you mean by phony attempts?" Patti asked above the chilly feeling surrounding her throat like clutching fingers.

"Hoaxes," the policeman warned. "Phone messages at night calling you to the hospital because a friend has been hurt. Anything designed to get you away from home. If you absolutely must go out at night, take the dog."

"I'll be careful. Thank you for coming." Patti ushered them out and beckoned to

Obsidian. He might be used to sleeping outdoors, but she needed his comforting presence inside tonight. She spread a clean blanket over the rug next to her bed and fell asleep with one hand on the dog's silky head.

Two days passed. Then three. Then five. Patti made a couple of routine flights. No opportunity arose for her to confront Scott with Charles's accusations. However, she used the time to observe him more closely than ever. Her heart insisted he must be innocent. Her head acknowledged there had to be some truth in the story. What had changed Scott from the laughing pilot she suspected he had once been to Stone Face Sloan, a man who maintained a certain distance even from Mike Parker, his closest friend?

A manila envelope with no return address left Patti more confused and torn than ever. It contained photocopies of newspaper clippings about a hearing several years earlier. Someone had painstakingly put them in chronological order, making a continued story. Patti curled up in front of a warm fire and started reading.

A chilling picture emerged. Scott, Charles Bradley, and two friends took off from Salt

Lake City in a chartered plane for post-Christmas skiing in Colorado. A freak storm roared out of nowhere and caught them. According to the news stories, Scott had also committed a cardinal sin. He failed to file a flight plan. In any event, the plane went down in the mountains. Only Scott and Charles survived. Scott remained unconscious until after the rescue crew arrived. Charles reported the other two died in the interim. He hinted that Scott's carelessness in not filing a flight plan had made the difference between life and death.

Scott testified Charles had been the one at the controls, but admitted he couldn't be sure. Neither could he account for the fact a flight plan hadn't been filed. A blow to the head followed by the unconsciousness had erased his memory of everything from before takeoff until the actual rescue.

Charles swore Scott lied, trying to weasel out of responsibility by attempting to shift blame. The hearing board found itself in a quandary. They had the word of one pilot against another, one a self-confessed amnesiac. They also wondered. How much difference did it make who piloted the plane? It was doubtful even the most skillful pilot could have successfully flown through such a storm.

Patti held her breath and picked up the last clipping. The headline read:

AIRPLANE CRASH KILLING TWO RULED TRAGIC ACCIDENT.

A capsulized account of the hearing followed as well as the statement neither of the surviving pilots was being held responsible.

No wonder the shadow of Scott's past lurked in his eyes. Patti's heart went out to him and she blinked back tears. Regardless of actual circumstances, a caring man like Stone Face would blame himself.

"I don't believe he'd overlook filing a flight plan," Patti murmured. She stared into the flames leaping high in the soot-blackened fireplace. "He was younger then, but Scott doesn't seem the type to be careless. What if he thought Charles filed the report, Lord?" Her heart pounded. "Suppose he left it to Charles, who overlooked it? Scott can't remember, but he must suspect. What about the girl and the nasty gossip?"

These were all knotty questions demanding answers. But no real answers came, only the throbbing of a fiercely partisan heart. *Scott Sloan might be grossly negligent,* but with every breath she took, Patti Thompson prayed for him to be innocent.

A few hours before Patti received her anonymous package, Stone Face sorted through his mail: mostly junk, a few bills, and a large manila envelope on the bottom of the stack. He opened it. A sheaf of papers cascaded out, like the ills of the world released when Pandora of mythical fame opened the forbidden box. A typed note on top read, "An identical set has been sent to Patti Thompson."

Scott grunted. "What on earth . . ." He tossed the note aside and froze. Spread out before him were photocopies: a complete collection of newspaper clippings recounting the tragedy he still hadn't been able to put in the past. He waited for the sick feeling that always accompanied memories of that terrible time. It came. So did the same assurance and peace he felt in the Bell Jet-Ranger that day long ago.

"Thank You, God," he fervently prayed. "For the first time in years, I feel free." Buoyed with strength he knew came from the Holy Spirit, Scott did something he had vowed never to do. He began at the earliest dated newspaper report and read straight through. When he finished the final clipping, he allowed it to fall to the floor, marveling. Tragedy remained in the happenings, yet from his present viewpoint, it felt as if it had happened to another man.

" 'Therefore if any man be in Christ, he is a new creature: old things are passed away; behold, all things are become new,' " Scott softly quoted. "Second Corinthians 5:17, King James."

Verse 18 swept into his mind. "And all things are of God, who hath reconciled us to himself by Jesus Christ, and hath given to us the ministry of reconciliation." Scott squirmed, wanting to savor his newfound freedom. Yet the words "ministry of reconciliation" refused to be sponged from his mind. Until he could forgive Charles for lying, if indeed the other pilot had sworn falsely, how could he expect to maintain the feeling of chains broken in his own life?

Scott had struggled to put the past behind, including his hatred of Charles. Yet no one on earth except Bradley would have reason to send a full account of the hearing to Patti Thompson. Had he done it in retaliation for the scene at the flying field? How would the nurse who won more of Scott's admiration with every shared flight receive the news her pilot had been accused of negligence?

Only one way to find out. He dialed Patti's number.

"It's Scott. If you haven't had dinner, are you free to go out?" He felt awkward and grinned to himself. Too many years had limped by since he had invited a female out for dinner.

"Why, yes. I am." She added in a troubled voice, "I need to talk with you."

"Concerning a packet you received from an anonymous donor?"

The telephone line faithfully reproduced her gasp. "How did you know?"

"Our mutual friend, question mark, included me in his information shower, along with a note informing me you were also a recipient of his generosity."

Patti didn't reply for a moment. When she did, her voice sounded brisk. Had she used the silence to recover from the shock of his invitation?

"Why don't I fix something here? It will be quieter than a restaurant and a better place to talk."

Scott made a counter offer. "Why don't I bring take-out? What do you like, Chinese? Ribs? There's a place here that serves lip-smacking ribs along with cornbread and coleslaw. Just one thing. You'll need a bib."

Some of the strain left her voice. "I don't

have a bib, but I have several rolls of paper towels."

"Good enough. I'll be there in about forty-five minutes."

"All right."

Scott put down the phone and headed for his closet. Why was the prospect of a business dinner with a fellow employee sending pleasurable anticipation through him? That's all it was, a business dinner. Nothing more. *Right,* a little voice mocked. "Then why are you reaching for your new western shirt?"

Scott laughed. "Why not?" he demanded while shaving, as much of God as of himself. "Once I have closure on the past, is there any reason why I shouldn't start looking for a life companion?"

"No reason at all," he told the man in the mirror. Strange how different his reverse image looked from the unsmiling reflection he usually saw while shaving or brushing his short, dark hair. This man looked alive, eager, ready to move on. The other had not.

All dressed up in the new navy shirt and gray slacks, Scott toyed with the idea of taking Patti some flowers. The corners of his mouth immediately turned down and he rejected the idea. Flowers went with courtship. He certainly wasn't courting his flight nurse. He ignored the skeptical "oh, yeah?" his little voice sneaked in before he could shut it down, and headed for the rib place. Their spicy aroma filled the Jeep on his way to the log cabin home.

When Scott rang the doorbell, Patti flung it wide. She looked downright delectable in a fluffy white sweater and dark slacks. One hand lay on a half-grown black lab's back.

"Quiet, Obsidian. Scott is a friend."

Scott stepped inside and waited while the dog sniffed and checked him out. "Don't you know better than to open the door without identifying callers?"

"Believe it or not, I could smell those ribs from the time you reached the bottom step," she told him. "Do you mind eating on trays? I never had a fireplace before, so I usually eat my meals in front of it."

"Sounds good to me. I spent a lot of time here with Dan. Not enough, though. Too busy, or thought I was." He looked around the colorful living room then followed her to the pine-paneled kitchen. "I see you haven't changed things. Don't most women rearrange the furniture? Seems I've heard they do." He laid the large package of food on a counter.

"I'm not most women," she told him pertly. "I like it the way it is. Good grief, you brought enough food to feed a bunk-house filled with cowboys!"

"Not quite. Did you ever see a cowboy eat? Or a pilot?" he teased.

By unspoken consent, neither brought up the subject uppermost on their minds until a great many crunchy brown ribs and most of the other food vanished. Scott trailed Patti to the kitchen again. He insisted on helping her wash and dry their few dishes.

"No need dirtying the dishwasher for them," he cheerfully told her. "It's kind of nice, being in a kitchen. I don't spend much time in the one in my apartment." He caught both the wistfulness in his voice and her quick glance. "Not that I can't cook," he hastily amended. "It just doesn't seem worthwhile when I'm alone."

"I know what you mean." Blue eyes soft, she smiled and hung her dishtowel to dry. When they settled back down in the living room, she went straight to the point. "What I read today shocked me."

Scott's hopes for Patti's trust in spite of the evidence died unborn. He leaped from his chair and stared down at her. Pain and disappointment harshened his voice.

"And knowing what I am, you don't want to fly with me."

CHAPTER 12

Knowing what I am, you don't want to fly with me.

Scott's words hit Patti like pieces of granite chipped from his stony face. Before she could answer, he turned on his heel and headed for the door. The rigid set of his shoulders betrayed the suffering she had inflicted by stating she'd been shocked at the newspaper accounts.

Don't let him go like this.

The little voice whispering in her soul freed Patti from the paralyzing impact of Scott's misinterpretation. She sprang from her seat, ran across the moss-like carpet, and clutched his arm.

"How can you think such a thing?" she choked out. "Scott Sloan, I'd trust you with my life!"

His gaze raked her face. Never had she been subject to such scrutiny. The dullness in his eyes gave way to disbelief. He shook off her hold and placed his hands on her shoulders.

"Do you mean that?" he grated.

She forced herself to meet his look squarely. "I don't lie."

Patti had seen many sunrises since coming to Montana. She remembered well the dawn hush, followed by a gentle hint of radiance in the sky then the eager sun bursting over a distant hill in all its glory. Scott Sloan's slow acceptance of her trust dawned the same way. She felt she had glimpsed the very soul of the man before her. The next instant, he gathered her into his arms and held her close. Not fiercely, or passionately, but as a shepherd cradles a lost lamb plucked from danger.

Twice in her life Patti had experienced what she believed was love. Never had she known the feeling of rightness, of coming home to the shelter where she belonged. She wanted to stay in Scott Sloan's arms forever. All too soon he released her. His forefinger tilted her chin upward. His lips sought and found hers in a tender kiss that ended almost before it began. Scott's arms dropped. If Patti lived to be a hundred, she knew she would never forget the expression in his eyes when he said, "Thank you, Patti," and walked out.

Blinded by the rush of tears she could not stop, she stood where she was. Someday they would talk again. Someday they would discuss blame, regret, all the things that must be cleared away in order for perfect healing to take place — just as wounds required the removal of dirt and foreign matter to avoid infection. For now, the gentle memory of Scott's kiss was all that mattered.

Scott Sloan drove away from the log cabin as if pursued by a Montana northern storm. He laughed mirthlessly. Neither his Jeep, nor the Bell Jet-Ranger could escape his love for Patti Thompson. He'd crash-landed permanently when she looked up at him with clear eyes and proclaimed her un-bounded trust in him.

"Trust is a long way from love," Scott grimly reminded himself. "Patti is only a few weeks past an engagement with Charles Bradley, Lord. The last thing she needs is pressure from me. Help me keep calm and steady." His mood lightened. "I'm not sorry I kissed her, though." Scott grinned and his pulse quickened. "A pilot needs to file his flight plan!"

The lyrics from one of the songs from *South Pacific* bubbled up and spilled out. Scott changed the words from "I'm in Love with a Wonderful Guy" to "wonderful girl" and sang all the words he could remember. A laugh of sheer exuberance escaped when he finished. *Rodgers and Hammerstein were right. A person in love really did feel high as a Fourth of July flag waving in the sky.*

Scott grinned at his flight of fancy. The soar from despair to the heights had certainly turned him poetic! How would Patti greet him the next time they met? Had she sensed his iron control when he kissed and released her? It hadn't been easy. In that precious moment, he had longed to wrap her in his arms and never let her go.

Scott's state of euphoria lasted all through the next week. He forced himself to act natural, but found it impossible to overlook the knowing expression on Mike Parker's face. Every time Scott carried on a conversation with their flight nurse, the Rescue Service owner fatuously grinned until his pilot wanted to punch him.

"Sorry," Scott apologized to God. "I'm just afraid he'll give me away before Patti is ready." His heart thumped at the thought. *What would it be like to come home to lighted windows, the log cabin — and Patti? Or with her?* Blood quickened in his veins at the thought. *Had God ever created a sweeter, truer woman?* Scott burned with remorse at his earlier suspicions of her.

Fresh doubt pressed hard on the heels of regret. He had saved a tidy sum, with the idea of buying a place of his own if he decided to remain in Kalispell. It paled in comparison with what Dan Davis had left Patti. Scott thought of Charles, pursuing Patti's inheritance as intently as the nurse. God forbid he should follow in Bradley's crooked trail by considering possessions!

Scott's mouth set in a grim line. "If she ever cares, Lord, there will have to be some kind of understanding between us. I can't see allowing her to provide for me, except maybe in sickness. I want to take care of her 'for better, for worse,' and all that." He laughed sheepishly. Why fly over mountain peaks before he reached their base? A single kiss, too brief for him to tell whether she responded, was a long way from discussing financial arrangements and wedding vows.

Along with Mike's curiosity and unspoken approval, Scott's heightened awareness also registered Patti Thompson's warm blush and her sidewise glances at him when she thought him absorbed in flying. Neither had mentioned the incriminating newspaper articles. Doing so meant raising the need to discuss what followed. Scott wasn't ready for that. Apparently, Patti wasn't, either.

They also didn't discuss the invisible something between them. Scott's promise to himself to remain calm and steady wavered again and again. The discipline of years and sense of fair play held him to his self-appointed course. He didn't want a wife — even Patti — on the rebound. If she showed signs of restlessness or mentioned leaving Montana, he would speak. Otherwise, his sense of fair play must keep him on his friendly, undemanding path.

It didn't keep him from dreaming. Or searching for telltale signs Patti might be learning to care. He failed miserably. Just when a look convinced him of Patti's fondness, her quick and natural interest in the country through which they flew robbed the moment of sentiment. Scott wished he knew more about women. He had thought himself in love a few times, but it always proved short-lived.

"There's a certain amount of glamour attached to the fact we fly missions of mercy," he reminded himself. He frowned. Once or twice a flight nurse had garbed him with hero-worship because of his job. He wanted no such adulation and had adroitly warded them off.

"At least Patti won't be influenced by my so-called uniform," Scott mused one evening after crawling into bed. "Denims and a baseball cap are a far cry from spit and polish, plus brass buttons. No relying on 'the fancy wrapper sells the goods.' I don't want Patti's love to be based on anything except who I am."

He yawned, turned off the light, and thanked God for another safe day of flying.

A few miles away, the object of Scott's soliloquy lay staring into the darkness. Why should she care that the tall pilot hadn't followed up on the kiss? Thank goodness he no longer maintained the glacial aloofness she had secretly battled early in their acquaintanceship. Now he treated her as a friend; no more, no less. *An improvement, but unsatisfactory,* Patti reluctantly admitted.

Had the kiss merely been an expression of gratitude for her spontaneous announcement of faith in him? She blushed from toes to hairline. Until or unless Scott pursued it, she must never let on how badly his touch had shaken her. Or that his gentle touch lingered in her mind and heart, erasing all others who had come before.

"You'd think you'd never been kissed before," she flouted. Honesty made her add, "I haven't like that, Lord. What shall I do? I'm terribly afraid this is for real. Will he ever care?" She fluffed her pillows in an attempt to sleep. Although her health had improved tremendously, she needed full strength to match the sometimes arduous demands of her job. *Too bad someone didn't invent a key to turn off the mind and all its worries at night.*

One glass of warm milk, two crackers, and a prayer later, Patti fell into a heavy sleep. The ringing of the phone awakened her. The large red numerals on her digital clock showed six-thirty in the morning. She shook her head to clear away the caterpillar-like fuzz in her brain.

"Hello?"

"Miss Thompson?"

"Yes."

"This is Dr. McArdle calling from . . ." The muffled voice named a local hospital. "Pilot Scott Sloan's Jeep collided with a pickup truck a short time ago. He was lucky and came out of it with some abrasions and a broken leg. He gave me your number and asked for you to come."

Patti's brain spun like a tumbleweed in high winds.

"Of course. Tell him I'll be there as soon as I can."

She hung up and grabbed the first clothing her hand touched when she opened the closet. She gave her teeth and short, blond hair a quick brush. No time to bother with lipstick. Once the shock of the call began to wear off, her heart sang a melody of joy: "He asked for me. Scott Sloan asked *me* to come."

Patti ran down the hall toward the front door. She unfastened the safety chain and stepped onto the porch. Obsidian, who again slept under her window now that no more had been heard of Charles Bradley, barked once and raced toward her. A morning chill struck her face and cleared most of the lingering shreds of sleep from her system. She rubbed her hands, wishing she had taken time to grab mittens. What difference did it make? Who cared about freezing fingers when Scott had asked her to come to the hospital?

She flew down the steps. Across the wide front yard toward the Bronco, ready and waiting for her ride to the hospital.

"No, you can't go with me," she told Obsidian when he joyously bounded after her.

The next instant, her foot hit a frosty patch and halted her wild rush. She sprawled on the ground with a solid thump to her left hip. It jolted her fully awake and mentally alert. Something lurked just outside her range of consciousness, something important, clamoring to be recognized and heeded.

Patti got up, rubbed her sore hip, and looked at the dog, a dark shadow in the pre-dawn. Snatches of a half-forgotten conversation returned, chilling, warning.

The police officer: "Don't fall for any phony attempts that can result in making you vulnerable. I'm not trying to terrify you. Just be careful."

Her own voice: "What kind of thing do you mean by phony attempts?" The chilly feeling surrounded her throat like clutching fingers.

The officer: "Hoaxes. Phone messages at night calling you to the hospital because a friend has been hurt. Anything designed to get you away from home. If you absolutely must go out at night, take the dog."

Patti turned and fled, backtracking like a fugitive trying to cover his trail. The heavy thud of footsteps beat behind her. She knew they only hammered in her mind. Otherwise, Obsidian would be barking his head off in pursuit instead of racing back up the steps and across the porch with her.

She blew on her icy fingers and warmed them enough to unlock the door. She almost fell inside, commanding Obsidian to follow.

The tranquillity of the room itself did more to settle her down than the relocked, rechained door when she sagged against its reassuring solidness. Doubt assailed her. There really was a Dr. McArdle at the hospital. She had met him briefly at the flight field. What if Scott really had been hurt and wanted her to come? Was she allowing foolish fear and cowardice to hold her back from answering his request?

Patti hurried to the phone and dialed.

"This is Nurse Thompson," she asked in her crispest, most businesslike voice. "I'd like to speak with either Dr. McArdle or Scott Sloan, a patient. I understand he was admitted a short time ago."

"Of course." An eternity later, a puzzled voice told her, "I'm sorry, but Dr. McArdle is at a medical convention in Helena and Scott Sloan isn't here. Actually, we haven't admitted anyone at all this morning."

Patti clutched the phone in a death grip. "Could he still be in emergency?"

"I'll check. Hold, please."

Another eternity crawled by before the nurse came back on the line.

"ER says no. Perhaps you have the wrong hospital." She sounded sympathetic.

I doubt it, Patti thought.

"Perhaps," she said. "Thanks, anyway."

She hung up.

Obsidian whined and rubbed his nose against her slacks. Patti had learned long ago how quickly he sensed her moods.

"It's all right, Boy," she reassured, knowing when she said it things were *not* all right. Someone wanted to frighten her badly enough to impersonate a doctor. Did the muffled voice that successfully masked the identity of the caller belong to Charles? She'd heard covering the mouthpiece of a phone with a handkerchief altered voices. Discovering Dr. McArdle's name and connection with the hospital would be child's play for a man as dedicated to trickery as Charles Bradley. Was he parked just up the road from her place as he had been that other time, waiting like a vengeful spider for her to fly into his web of deceit?

Fed up with the blond pilot and his ruses, Patti came to a quick decision. The tempo of her heartbeat increased, but she determinedly punched in Scott Sloan's phone number for the very first time. He answered on the third ring.

Her hand felt sweaty on the phone.

"This is Patti. I hope I didn't wake you."

"You didn't."

How could he sound so casual when every nerve in her body twanged?

"I hate to bother you, but I had to check. Are you all right?"

"Of course I'm all right. Why?"

Good grief, does he think I'm some on-his-trail female inventing excuses to call him at home? The thought steadied Patti.

"Someone posing as Dr. McArdle called me from the hospital. He said you had been hurt, and —"

He cut her off. "I'm on my way."

Patti put down the phone and stared at Obsidian.

"Well! He doesn't waste any more words than Ma Hoff." She took off her jacket and went to hang it up. A glimpse of the disheveled nurse in her bedroom mirror made her groan. She changed to clean pants and put the others to soak, then bathed her face and hands before brushing her hair again.

By the time Scott arrived, Patti's singing teakettle performed its merriest tune.

"Sorry I don't have coffee," she apologized. "It always smells so good and tastes so bad. I have boiling water, chocolate and herbal tea."

"Chocolate's fine. I'm not that much into coffee," Scott told her.

Patti sensed his impatience, curbed for the sake of courtesy until she prepared the hot drinks and they sat facing each other across the table in the pine-paneled dining room. Obsidian lay close to her chair.

"The call awakened me. I was really out of it, since it took me a long time last night to get to sleep."

"Why?" Scott barked. His dark gaze demanded the truth, the whole truth, and nothing but the truth; exactly what she couldn't tell him! Patti relaxed when he added, "Has Bradley been up to something? I mean, before now. It sounds like one of his tricks."

"Not that I know of." Patti heaved a secret sigh of relief. She had no intention of telling Stone Face he, not Charles, was the source of her sleeplessness. She rushed on, failing to exercise caution because of her narrow escape. "The bogus Dr. McArdle said you were asking for me. I tossed on clothes, got halfway to the Bronco, and —"

"You rushed out before daylight because I supposedly sent for you?"

"Yes."

The word hung in the air.

Scott drew a shaken breath. Patti risked a look directly into his eyes. The softest light she had ever seen in the dark depths shone like a beacon before he collected himself and gruffly ordered, "Go on."

"I slipped on frosty grass." She ruefully

218

rubbed her sore hip. "The fall and Obsidian brought me to my senses." She repeated the police officer's warning she had remembered and finished by saying, "I came back inside and called the hospital. Dr. McArdle wasn't there. Neither were you."

"Thank God you didn't fall for the hoax." Scott reached across the table and grabbed her hand in his long, supple fingers. "Have you called the police?"

"Not yet. I don't see what they can do about it," Patti reflected.

He glanced at the window.

"It will be light enough soon for them to do some checking. Patti, are you holding anything back?"

She shook her head. "No. I already told the police the way Charles behaved that time he came here and Obsidian acted so unfriendly."

"What time?" Scott's voice cracked like a pistol. "Why didn't you tell me?"

She sat very still. How could she admit Charles's threat had grown out of her reaction to his maligning Scott? A long moment followed while reluctance and honesty fought. Honesty won. Patti chose her words carefully.

"Charles didn't want me to fly with you. He talked about you —" She stopped and steadied her voice. "He asked me to let him in so he could tell me the rest of the story. I told him if I wanted to hear it, I'd ask you."

The same light Patti had seen in Scott's eyes when she cried out her faith in him returned. He reached across the table and took her cold hands in his. Patti saw a tiny pulse beating in his temple. She tightened her grip on his strong hands and swayed toward him. To her amazement, the light went out in his eyes. Scott dropped her hands and leaned back.

"Not now, Patti."

She scorched with shame. How could she have allowed herself to betray the newly awakened love that longed for his protecting arms? She had been right. Stone Face cared nothing for her as a woman. His kiss had been nothing more than gratitude for her trust.

She jerked back. The quick movement brought Obsidian's ears up and he whined.

"It's all right," Patti told him. She patted his head and hesitated. Should she open the wound inflicted by Charles Bradley that had been festering inside her? Yes. Exposing it was the only way to start the healing process. "Sorry. You must think me as brazen as the woman Charles mentioned."

Scott's face went deathly white.

"Woman?" he asked in a ragged voice.

"He said you came between him and a girl he was trying to protect from nasty gossip," Patti faltered. Why had she ever brought it up?

"And you believed him."

His gaze burned into her like a red-hot branding iron. Patti felt she had been seared to the soul. She closed her eyes, shot up a desperate prayer for guidance, then forced herself to look Scott full in the face.

"Not if you tell me differently."

The glacial ice encasing Stone Face gradually melted and trickled away. Warmth flowed into his face once more.

"Thank you," he quietly said. "Yes, there was a girl. Thank God it's not a bedtime story. Bradley was wild about her. She loved one of the men who died in the crash." He paused. "It didn't matter to Bradley that she cared nothing for him. He hounded her, while pretending to be her fiancé's friend." Scott's steady gaze never left Patti's face. "The same kind of thing he is doing to you."

She shivered and crossed her arms over her chest.

"She came to me, afraid of what her fiancé might do when he learned Bradley was persecuting her. I warned Charles to back off or the girl would bring him up on harassment charges. I had observed enough to testify against him. Bradley retaliated by starting some pretty ugly rumors about us." A faint smile crossed his lips. "Fortunately, people knew me. They also knew Bradley."

Suspicion attacked like the enemy at dawn. Patti leaned forward, Scott's withdrawal from her forgotten. A question hovered on her lips, the way the Bell Jet-Ranger hovered before setting down. Instinct shouted a piece of the puzzle crucial to finding the truth about the tragic plane crash lay in Scott's answer.

Chapter 13

"Scott." Patti caught her lower lip between her teeth. "Did you threaten to testify about Charles Bradley's harassment before or after the plane crash?"

"Before." His unreadable expression told her nothing.

"That's it!" She shoved her chair back from the dining room table and stood. "He must have set you up so if it ever came to trial, you'd be discredited."

"I've always believed that but I can't prove it." Scott also rose, dark eyes appealing. "Until I do, and until we can get Charles Bradley and his evil schemes out of our lives, much as I'd like to, we can't move on."

Patti felt blood rush into her face until she felt she might suffocate. He hadn't rejected her!

"Then that's why you . . ." She bit her tongue instead of speaking the rest of the sentence: "didn't respond when I betrayed myself."

"Yes." He reverted from Scott Sloan to Stone Face, except his lips twitched and spoiled the effect. "Now I suggest we notify the police."

The same officers came but had no way to trace the phone call.

"We know where Charles Bradley is staying," they assured Patti when she told them she believed he had impersonated Dr. McArdle. "He has also accepted a temporary job with a charter service, flying hunting and hiking parties into the mountains."

"I hope we never run into him." Scott gave a short laugh. "I'd be tempted to flatten the guy."

"Don't. We've been doing some checking into his past."

"And?" Patti's nerves screamed.

"Let's just say he isn't a pleasant guy when he doesn't get his own way," the second officer warned. "Keep us informed if anything else unusual happens, and don't tangle with Bradley. His smooth, All-American-boy image is only a thin crust over a boiling volcano. We have the feeling it's only a matter of time until he explodes. You don't want to be around if or when it happens."

His counterpart sighed. "It's too bad we can't haul him in, but we don't have proof Bradley has broken any laws so far. Until he does, we're stuck."

A wave of helplessness threatened to swamp Patti. "I understand, but it doesn't make me feel any better."

The officers looked around the comfortable room, then at Obsidian.

"You might consider checking into a motel, although you're probably safe enough here with the dog."

"The Hoffs would be glad to have you at the Running H, but driving in takes too much time if we're on a hurry-up call," Scott reminded. "So does coming to get you in the chopper."

Iron entered Patti's backbone. She set her lips in a stubborn line. "I refuse to be intimidated and driven from my home. Besides, the danger isn't here. It's somewhere out there." She waved toward the window.

The officers warned her to be careful and departed. She and Scott walked to the road and watched the police car stop a short distance from Patti's driveway.

"Looking for tire tracks," she murmured.

To her disappointment, they gave no indication of their findings. When they completed their leisurely examination, they simply nodded to the watching couple and drove away.

"Well, that's that." Scott smiled at Patti. Her heart beat fast at the look in his eyes. "I'm heading home to shower and change." He rubbed one hand over the dark shadow on chin and cheeks. "Shave, too. At least I hope I have time before Mike calls us. See you later."

"See you," she called when he crawled in the Jeep and left. Then, "Come on, Obsidian. I need a bath, too. I hope things stay quiet for a time. A long time."

For a few days, it appeared Patti's wish had been granted. She flew two routine missions with Scott and faithfully reported all remained calm. Charles Bradley had neither turned up nor attempted another fright tactic.

October 30 came, clear and bright. The next day, the colorful month exited in a rainstorm as gray as steam from a fairy-tale witch's cauldron. The short glimpses of blue sky and clearing showed fresh snow on distant peaks.

November 1 dawned with overcast skies. Lowering clouds warned of rain. The chill in the air hinted of possible snow at Kalispell, as well as in the mountains.

Mike Parker's call caught Patti at her easel. True to her vow, she used much of her free time drawing and painting. She could see the improvement in her work with every completed project. Mike's sober voice effectively changed her from would-be artist to competent rescue nurse.

"We need you. There's a small plane down in the mountains. Probably an inexperienced pilot who got caught in a down draft. Or one who had been drinking." He sighed. "No sense wasting time talking about it. Wear warm clothes, boots, and don't forget your sheepskin-lined jacket. You may need it."

Patti put on thermal underwear under her favorite denim outfit and red turtleneck. She donned thick socks, her boots, and caught up her red bandanna, heavy lined gloves, and warm jacket.

"I feel ten pounds heavier," she told Scott at the hangar. She took in his garb similar to her own. "We look like the Bobbsey Twins, except for your black turtleneck and baseball cap."

"Thanks, but I have something in mind other than being your twin," he teased.

The ready-to-fly nurse felt red flags wave in her face. Although Scott couldn't always control the expression in his eyes, he seldom let himself off the leash enough for such a remark. It set butterflies quivering in her rib cage.

The next instant, he became all business.

"We're not sure what we'll find. The radio message was garbled. Thank God it didn't fade out until we learned the location." He glanced at her medical bag. Hard wear and contact with rough ground gave it a worn look. "Do you have everything you need?"

"Yes." She trotted with him to the waiting Bell Jet-Ranger and climbed inside. She noticed Scott's furtive glance at the horizon. "Is it going to storm?"

"Probably. Don't worry. If all goes well, we'll get to the downed plane, collect pilot and passengers, and be back before it amounts to anything. Piece of cake." He sent her a reassuring smile and lifted off.

They had no trouble finding the downed plane. A little over an hour later, they discovered the small charter plane sprawled like a broken toy near the bottom of a wide canyon. A stream tumbled by a few yards from the wreckage. Patti marveled again at the expert way Scott found and landed on a spot of level ground she hadn't believed large enough to hold them.

He slipped from his harness.

"Let's get them and get out of here."

Patti followed his gaze to the threatening sky. It looked worse than when they had left Kalispell. She grabbed her medical bag and headed for the wrecked plane.

One look at the scene before her exploded Scott's piece-of-cake theory. Four men in various states of shock and injury had managed to crawl a little distance from the wreckage. Four men plus Patti and Scott equaled six. The Bell Jet-Ranger only held five.

"We'll have to double up, somehow cram four into the back," she whispered to herself. A hasty examination of the first crash victim crumbled her hope. His terribly twisted knee required an inflatable cast to immobilize it for the flight back. Patti tried to ignore the all-gone feeling that settled in her stomach. She checked the other two passengers and sighed with relief. They showed signs of shock, but had sustained no serious injuries.

An exclamation from Scott sent her hurrying to the pilot, doubled over in the grotesque position on the ground where he had evidently fallen when he crawled from the plane. Semi-conscious, his breathing tainted the wintry mountain air with the smell of liquor. Blood stained his face, oozing from a cut on one cheek.

Patti's heart leap-frogged to her throat. "Charles?"

"Yes." Scott moved aside to allow Patti better access. "How is he?"

"Stunned." She ran expert hands over the injured man's limbs. "No sign of broken bones. You need to get him and the others to a hospital right away."

Patti set her lips. "I have to put an inflatable cast on one man's leg. It's not going to be easy to get all of them into the chopper."

Scott didn't pretend to misunderstand her use of the word "them." His face twisted and he suddenly looked old.

"If only you could fly the bird! You can't." Color drained from his cheeks until they resembled dirty snow. "Patti, our first duty and loyalty is to those we serve."

"I know." She fought fear of what lay ahead and forced herself to raise her chin. "The sooner you leave, the quicker you'll be back." She resolutely ignored the darkening sky and managed a strangled laugh. "I always wondered whether I'd get any use out of the survival pack. I guess this is when I find out."

"I'll put up the tent and start a fire while you do first aid," he told her.

What felt like an eternity later, but was actually an incredibly short period of time,

Scott led Patti into the assembled tent away from possible curious stares.

"It tears me apart to leave," he whispered. "I promise before God to come back for you. Three hours should do it." He pointed to a pile of wood he'd stacked inside the tent. "It's damp from yesterday's downpour, so keep piling it on the fire I built. The heat will dry it enough to burn. Except when you're feeding the fire, stay in the tent. Use the space blankets if you can't keep warm enough from the fire. There's food if you get hungry." He paused. "Here's something to think about until I come back." He gathered her into his strong arms, tilted her chin, and kissed her.

Patti felt the same feeling of all-rightness she had before. Only this time Scott did not pull away so soon. She sensed his reluctance to release her even when he raised his head and said, "Ironic, isn't it? Of all the pilots flying in Montana, it would be Bradley. Maybe God is trying to tell us something."

Patti thought of his words long after the whir of the chopper echoed from mountain to canyon and died. Did things really just happen? What were the odds against Scott and her being sent to rescue Charles Bradley? The call for help could easily have gone elsewhere. Even if it came to Mike Parker, he had other pilot/nurse teams. Was Scott right? Did God have a lesson in all this?

"If you do, I sure don't know what it is, Lord." Patti hastily added more branches to the fire. With Scott's departure, it had turned sullen and smoldered instead of burning brightly. She waited to make sure it continued burning and went back into the tent.

"At least Scott won't have any trouble finding me again." Patti giggled. It sounded loud in the silence, but she felt better. "Here I sit like the wife in Peter Pumpkin Eater's pumpkin shell."

She checked her watch. Her eyes widened in disbelief. Had it stopped? Surely more than fifteen minutes had passed since Scott tucked her in the pumpkin orange tent and flew away! Patti held the watch to her ear. Its rhythmic ticking faithfully counted off the seconds. Each felt like an hour.

"Lord, how am I going to stand being alone in the mountains for nearly three more hours?"

She began to repeat favorite Scriptures, ending with "God is our refuge and strength, a very present help in trouble." Of course! Hadn't God created the very mountains in which He permitted her to be left behind? He must have had a reason. Her part was to simply trust him and wait for Scott.

An hour limped by. Wisps of fog united and wove a gray flannel blanket Patti's keen vision found hard to penetrate. Fear turned her mouth metallic. Her prayers for Scott's return changed to a frantic plea he wouldn't attempt to come back until the weather lifted.

"He knows I'm all right, Lord," she prayed. Yet memory of Scott saying "I promise before God to come back for you" robbed her of even that comfort.

A second hour passed. The murk danced and swirled with occasional breaks. Patti faithfully fed the sulky fire. What would she do when the wood ran out? It would surely do so if Scott were delayed or she had to stay overnight. Was the utility knife in the survival pack strong enough for her to cut more? Could she find downed branches and brush? She forced herself to leave the security of her makeshift camp. Triumph sprang to her eyes when she found storm-broken trees. A great pile of branches lay at the foot of a stark, lightning-scarred snag. Her heavily gloved hands tore at them. She gathered an enormous pile, encircled it with her arms, and staggered back to her haven. Load after load she carried, until the treacherous fog threatened to lure her into losing her direction if she strayed farther.

Patti tingled with the exercise and discovered she was ravenous. Trips to the bubbling stream nearby resulted in a goodly supply of water. She longed to throw herself down on the bank of the stream and drink her fill, but remembered the need to purify it before drinking. She used a water purification tablet according to directions in the survival manual, then prepared a cup of hot tea. Never had anything tasted better than it and the tropical chocolate bar she wolfed down. That and the tea would be her lunch. She must hoard her provisions against the possibility fog kept Scott from making it back. Lonesome, more frightened for Scott than herself, Patti repeated every comforting Scripture she could remember. It was her only shield against terror until the pilot she loved safely returned.

Scott Sloan gritted his teeth. Never had a trip to home base flown on such leaden wings. At first, the three injured plane passengers said little. Charles Bradley more than made up for it. He had regained consciousness enough to recognize Scott for a moment, but not enough to differentiate between the recent plane crash and the one long ago. He babbled about getting revenge by failing to file a flight plan and swearing Sloan had been at the controls instead of him.

Although the day had darkened even more, Scott felt the sun rise in his soul. He hadn't been responsible for the death of those two men. *Thank God!*

The youngest-looking passenger caught part of Charles's mumbling. "This jerk didn't file a plan? What is he, crazy? If we hadn't sent a message before the radio conked out, we'd still be back there with a downed plane!"

"He's talking about another flight," Scott explained. "Remember what he says, will you? I took the heat for him failing to follow orders."

"I'll remember all right," the man grimly said. "Bradley's going to lose his pilot's license over this. None of us realized he'd been drinking until he took off. We insisted he turn back. He refused. Said one drink made him more alert. It's a wonder we didn't all die in the crash."

"What exactly happened?" Scott wanted to know. "Did a down draft pull you into the canyon?"

"Are you kidding?" The passenger sounded incredulous. "Bradley's judgment must have been impaired by booze. He veered right. The wing evidently hit the rock wall. Next thing I knew, we were going down." He soberly added, "Hard to believe any of us are alive. Lucky, I guess, or someone watching out for us."

"You'd better believe it," Scott agreed.

"Leaving the nurse behind was rotten," the man observed. "We should have left Bradley, but she wouldn't stand for it. Or for any of us staying. I volunteered. What a woman! Is she married?"

"No, but she's going to be." Scott couldn't keep a broad grin from stretching across his face. "To me." *I hope,* he mentally added.

"Some guys have all the luck! Say, are you going to be able to go back for her? It's getting pretty ugly out there."

"I'm going." Scott folded his lips shut and concentrated on his flying. The talkative passenger took the silent hint and subsided.

An hour later, Scott and Mike Parker watched the ambulance take the crash victims away.

"Thank God they aren't all dead," Mike fervently breathed. Scott had filled him in while unloading his passengers. He squinted at the blackening sky. "Maybe you'd better hold off and see if this stuff lifts."

"Not on your life. Patti's waiting. I vowed

before God to come for her."

"She'll wait a lot longer if you don't make it," Mike retorted. He folded his arms across his paunch. "I can order you not to go, for your own good. I won't."

His pudgy hand shot out and gripped Scott's with surprising strength. "I knew Patti Thompson would be like this."

Scott squeezed Mike's hand until the other man winced, then climbed back into the Bell Jet-Ranger and began the most important mercy mission of his life.

Weather worsened and snarled warnings to the unwary on that endless flight. "Turn back. Turn back." Scott ignored the voice and flew on. Patches of fog appeared. A light wind followed, tossing the fog into writhing, snakelike banners. When he entered the canyon a few miles from his destination, the fog thickened into gray globs, decreasing visibility. Scott peered between them, gauging distance. He had to set down where he had before.

A vivid thrust of red he recognized as an aerial flare cut through the fog and brought an approving grunt. Patti must have heard the chopper and set off the flare.

"Smart girl. Okay, Sloan. Time to take this bird down." A fog patch moved, making a hole in the murk. Scott loosened his shoulder harness, leaned forward to see better, and began his descent. He wouldn't make the same spot, but could hover and see exactly where he was.

A heartbeat later, the stark, lightning-scarred snag where Patti had gathered fuel for her fire appeared in the gloom. The capricious wind chose the worst moment possible to show its power. It picked up, gusted, and blew the Bell Jet-Ranger straight toward the snag. The main rotor blade hit the dead tree with a resounding smack. The impact flipped the chopper on its side.

Scott's loosened shoulder harness couldn't restrain him enough to keep him from pitching forward when the blade slammed into the snag. His head made contact with something hard, leaving him dazed, unable to think clearly.

A short time earlier, Patti Thompson had roused from her study of the survival manual. She hadn't realized how tense she'd been until her muscles and nerves began to unknot at the distant sound of a chopper. Yet fear did not retreat. The wavering fog spelled danger. Patti grabbed a red aerial flare and ran outside. Long experience with the helicopter's deafening "clackety-clack" told her the best moment to set off the flare. Its welcome glow when it shot skyward calmed her.

Patti caught a glimpse of the familiar white chopper through the fog. She longed to race toward it but knew better. Until it settled down like a broody hen over her chicks, people on the ground needed to keep a safe distance. Down, down — Patti gasped in horror when the descending chopper swayed in the wind. Her cry of protest mingled with the heart-stopping sound of the rotor blade striking the snag. The next instant, the chopper flipped on its side.

"No, God!" Patti screamed. She rushed forward. The smell of leaking fuel sent a fresh wave of terror through her. *Would the chopper catch fire? Explode?* The gruesome thought lent the strength she needed to wrench open the helicopter door, help Scott out, and yell, "We have to get away from the chopper." Inch by inch, foot by foot, she led him past the fire she had faithfully kept going and into the tent.

"I have to check you over. Standard operating procedure," she ordered.

It brought a grin. "I'm okay except for this." He touched his forehead.

"I'll decide that." She peered into his eyes. "Good. No signs of concussion. Did you lose consciousness at all?"

"No." He caught her hands. "Thanks for hauling me out. I was pretty dazed."

A crackling sound caught Patti's attention. She freed one hand and pointed through the open tent flap at the helicopter. Tongues of flame grew higher every minute.

"I was afraid it would explode before I could get you out."

Scott shook his head. "Choppers are powered by jet kerosene. A fuel line breaks and puts gas on the hot engine. Fire starts in the back part of the fuselage, just behind the back seat." A worry line made an inverted V between his dark eyebrows. "We're in a spot," he told her. "We have no radio contact. Our ELT — Emergency Locator Transmitter — would have sent a signal the chopper has crashed, but we can't expect help as long as the fog holds."

Dread of what lay ahead caught Patti's throat in a death grip. Yet when she looked into Scott's shadowed face, she felt a renewal of courage.

"We're alive and together, aren't we? Nothing else matters." The expression in his eyes before he opened his arms and she flew into them echoed her words.

CHAPTER 14

"I need to level with you," Scott told Patti after a meager meal of hot soup and granola bars. "You aren't a child. You have the right to know what we're up against. Normally, staying put is the best thing for crash survivors. We may not have that option. It all depends on the weather." A muscle twitched in Scott's cheek and he looked deep into her blue eyes. "You once said you would trust me with your life. Does it still hold?"

Patti answered the pleading in his voice rather than the question.

"Yes."

A dark red tide swept into the pilot's strained face. "That's all I need to know. Actually, there is one thing more." He paused and measured her with his dark gaze. He grinned and asked, "Are you a romantic?"

She blinked at the sudden change of

subject. "A romantic?"

Sparkles danced in his eyes. "Is there an echo in here? You know what I mean. Are you the kind of girl who dreams of receiving marriage proposals in a rose garden, or while watching a spectacular sunset?"

Unable to believe her own ears, Patti eyed him suspiciously. She tried to control the red tide she felt sweep up from the collar of her sheepskin-lined jacket. She put her hands on her hips.

"Why do you care, especially now?"

Scott's grin faded. He sounded strangely humble when he said in a low voice, "I just wondered how you'd feel about a guy who loves you so much he would propose in an orange survival tent."

He briefed her on Charles's semi-conscious ramblings and closed by saying, "I'm finally free from guilt and ready to move on. I want you to know you're the only woman in the world for me, just in case."

His last foreboding words couldn't drown the happiness Patti's heart radiated to every part of her body.

"Pumpkin shell," she muttered.

"What?!" Scott gaped as if she had gone stark, staring mad.

Patti felt like a fool. How could she have

answered him that way?

"I–I'm sorry. It's just that when you left I kept thinking of the nursery rhyme about Peter who put his wife in a pumpkin shell and 'kept her very well.' " She put one hand to her burning face and fervently wished he'd do something other than stand there looking like the Stone Face she first met!

A full minute passed before laughter spilled from Scott like a waterfall cascading over a rocky cliff to the bottom of a ravine.

"Never in *my* wildest dreams did I suspect the girl I'm asking to share my life would answer like this!" he said when he caught his breath enough to speak. "I can't promise you a pumpkin shell. Just a pretty good pilot who loves you second only to God. Will you, Patricia, take this man . . ."

"I will," she whispered. Patti wrapped her arms around Scott and raised her face for his kiss. Someday after they fought the elements and won, she would repeat that promise in the presence of family and friends. Yet Patti's heart pumped with secret knowledge. White lace and wedding vows could never be more precious or binding than the pledge made in a pumpkin shell tent with only God and a worsening storm as witnesses. It accepted all the rest: better and worse; richer and poorer; sickness and health; as long as they both should live.

"I'm sorry I don't have a ring for you," Scott told her when he finally released her and stepped back. "We'll take care of it first thing when we get back."

Patti's glow of happiness dimmed. Contrary to the old cliché, people did not live on love, especially in the treacherous Big Sky Country with winter lurking around the corners of the tent.

"If the weather forces us to leave, where can we go?" she asked. "Thank God you know this country better than I."

Scott nodded. "There's a ramshackle cabin about ten miles from here. I've flown over it. We follow the stream up the canyon until we can find a good place to climb out. It's beyond me why anyone would build his perch partway up a canyon wall instead of closer to water. Afraid of flooding, maybe. Anyway, we won't have trouble finding it. We also have the survival pack compass."

"How will the rescue chopper know where to find us?"

Scott grinned, tore a blank sheet from the back of the survival manual, and wrote in large letters: GONE TO CHARLEY'S FOLLY.

"I'll post it on the remains of the Bell Jet-Ranger. Mike or any pilot he sends will know exactly where to find us. All of us who fly this region make it a point to know where we can find shelter in case we need it."

"Why is the shack called Charley's Folly?" Patti wanted to know.

"It happened before I came to Kalispell, but according to the story, a crazy old coot named Charley built the shack. Said he was going to find gold. Charley claimed to be over a hundred years old, and looked it! Folks only saw him when he stumbled into nearby towns for staples: salt, flour, sugar, coffee. Otherwise, he pretty much lived off the land." Scott smiled. "Game wardens left him alone. They weren't as careful in those days. Besides, just getting to his place meant a long, hard trek."

"What a strange story. Like something from the Old West," Patti burst out.

Scott lowered his voice to a mysterious whisper. "You haven't heard the beginning of strange! All of a sudden, Charley stopped coming in for grub."

Patti clasped her hands together and leaned forward.

"Did he die?"

"No one knows. He simply vanished. Disappeared. Vamoosed." Patti could tell Scott was enjoying her full attention. He continued, "A couple of smart guys from Kalispell figured Charley might have found gold; maybe hid it in his cabin and then fell over a cliff. Or died of old age somewhere out in the woods. They searched the place. Everything looked like the owner had just up and walked away. Dishes on the table. Clothing on hooks. An open Bible with pages falling apart next to a rickety cot. The get-rich-quick guys called the place Charley's Folly. The name stuck."

"It's sad to think the man died alone in the wilderness," Patti murmured.

"Why?" Scott sounded genuinely surprised. "That's how he lived. What more fitting place for him to die?" His gaze softened. "The Bible by the cot shows Charley wasn't as crazy as folks thought. It had seen a lot of hard use to be in the condition the men found it. They left it where it was. It may be there yet."

"I hope so." The thought of a Bible, worn and aged as it might be, offered one bright spot of welcome to what Patti knew must surely be a hovel.

"Enough stories," Scott told her. "Try and get some sleep."

"I've never been more wide awake," she protested.

He dropped a kiss on her forehead. "Obey the pilot in command. He's going to replenish the fire. Good thing you dragged in all those tree limbs for fuel." He reached for an armful and hauled them to the fire.

To Patti's utter amazement, she fell asleep before he returned. She roused twice in the night, saw Scott's comforting dark bulk, and went back to sleep. She awoke to a demanding hand on her shoulder and a white-shrouded world.

"Wake up, Patti. We have to get out of here. Now, while we still can."

The urgency in his voice chased away tatters of sleep. Stiff and sore from her unaccustomed bed, she stretched and rubbed kinks from her arms and legs. She tried to lighten the tension emanating from Scott.

"What? No breakfast in bed?"

He didn't take time to respond to her sally. "It snowed three inches last night. If the sky's any indication, we're in for more. I only pray it will hold off until we reach Charley's Folly." He handed her a cup of hot, sweetened tea and half of a chocolate bar. "Sorry, but we need to hoard our rations."

"It's all right. Thanks." The tea warmed Patti's stomach. She stepped from the tent. Snow had mercifully shrouded part of the Bell Jet-Ranger's remains. After one quick glance, Patti avoided looking in its direction. So many happy, serving hours and memories were connected with the chopper!

Stop standing here like a ninny and get busy, she sharply ordered herself. *The last thing Scott needs on this expedition is a helpless female moping around and shedding tears over a downed helicopter.*

Scott expertly repacked the survival pack. He made no attempt to include the wet tent, but folded it into a compact package. Patti admired the way his deft hands cleverly roped pack, tent, filled water container, and the two canteens together in a yoke-like arrangement he could carry on his back.

"Can you manage your medical bag?" he asked.

"Yes. It's like an extension of my arm." Patti wiggled her fingers more firmly into her gloves, adjusted her bandanna, and picked up the lifesaving medical bag. Its familiar weight comforted her. At least she and Scott were well equipped.

Before they started out, they joined hands. Scott's prayer was simple, terse. "Lord, we need Your help. Guide us to Charley's Folly and help us overcome obstacles on the way. We thank and praise You in Jesus' name, amen."

"Amen," Patti whispered. She refused to

allow herself to conjure up those obstacles Scott knew lay ahead but kept to himself.

They found the going fairly easy for the first mile. After that, it became a nightmare. Gully-washers since Scott flew over the area had changed the course of the stream, leaving debris and boulders to surmount. At first, Patti clambered over them as nimbly as the mountain goat that surveyed her on her very first rescue mission. Yet each succeeding barrier drained her of a little more energy. She laughed to hide the growling of a stomach in need of food. Oh, for a plate of those crunchy brown ribs Scott had brought to her log cabin!

"Concentrate on something else," she muttered, making sure he didn't hear her. "Wishing for the moon — or crunchy ribs — won't get us to Charley's Folly any sooner." Patti grinned to herself. Thinking about food had one advantage: It made her mouth water and relieved its dryness.

Minutes struggled into an hour. Then two. Then three. If they had been on flat ground, the travelers would have already reached their destination. The waiting snow allowed them no leeway, no time extension. A few lazy flakes warned them to take cover. There was none.

They plodded ahead. Patti felt as if she

had been ascending and descending log jams and piles of boulders forever. A slight bend in the trail brought the hikers right up against the highest jam yet. Mustering strength, Patti painstakingly followed Scott over it, only to find the space between stream and canyon wall had narrowed to less than two feet! A little farther, it dwindled even more. When its width became less than eight inches, Scott called a halt.

"It's not the best place to climb, but we don't have a choice." He pointed to a structure above them and a little to the left. A steep and tipsy trail zigzagged up to it from the stream. Patti strained to see through the increasing snowflakes.

Scott laid down his burdens and untied the rope from his hastily assembled carrying contraption. He rooted matches from the survival pack and stuffed them in his jacket pocket.

"The trail is steep and may be slippery from the snow." He sounded as casual as though reciting a poem. "We won't take any chances." He tied the rope around her waist, then his own. "Leave the medical bag here. I'll come back for it and the other stuff. Keep the rope slack, in case I slip. If you start to fall, dig in fingers, toes, and hang on. I won't let you drop."

Patti couldn't have held back her giggle if her life depended on it.

"All this and a course in mountain climbing, too," she told him.

Scott flashed her an appreciative grin. "All this and the Charley's Folly Hilton waiting on top. May I show Madame Thompson to her room?"

Laughter released a fresh thrust of energy. Patti started up the crooked trail, leaving the rope slack between them as ordered. Once her boot hit a concealed patch of ice and she lost her footing. The rope tightened. She dug fingers and toes into the earth. Scott held her steady and a moment later, she scrambled forward.

They successfully navigated the final turns in the crazily tilted path. Patti stopped to catch her breath and gazed at her temporary home away from home.

Scott grinned. "We won't spend our honeymoon here, but it's shelter."

"Barely." Patti looked at the precariously perched hut that looked as if it had started out as a log cabin a century or two before. Various and sundry nailed-on pieces of wood patched it. Rough boards over frayed canvas outlined window openings. She giggled. "It resembles a crazy quilt my great-grandmother made. Why hasn't it blown away?"

Scott examined the structure more closely. "No danger of that. Charley built his Folly to withstand Montana blizzards and northers. Care to step inside?"

"Not really." She laughed again, this time to cover the quaver in her voice. Entering this squalid shack wouldn't be easy. "You go first. A critter or two may be occupying the bridal suite."

Scott gave two hard jerks and opened the creaking, weather-swollen door. He lit a match and grunted.

"Good. There are a few ancient candle stubs." He lighted one and made a face at Patti, who hesitated in the open doorway. "Whew! It's musty in here. I'd say we need to do some housecleaning."

She forced herself to step inside and look around. Housecleaning? Where should they start? With the dusty, web-covered ceiling and walls? The rickety looking sheet-iron stove, leaning table and two tipsy chairs? The floor, inches deep with dirt? The falling-down cot, whose filthy blankets partially covered boughs that had long since lost their needles? Charley's Bible still lay by the cot.

Don't let Scott know how appalled you are.

He has enough to worry about without your failing to be a good sport. So God didn't provide a Hilton. As Scott said, it's shelter.

Patti squared her slim shoulders. Her chin raised. She forced snap into her voice and a sparkle into her eyes.

"Well! The sooner we start, the sooner we'll be through." She firmly squashed the sardonic little whisper in her heart, *"Oh, yeah?"*

"Fire first." Scott examined the stove, shook the stovepipe to make sure it hadn't rusted into a falling-down state, and grunted again. "Thank God it's serviceable."

A quick search of the cabin disclosed a crumpled newspaper. Scott crumpled it, stopped long enough to kiss Patti's upturned nose, and went back outside. Before despair over the condition of Charley's Folly had time to clutch her again, Scott returned, carrying an armload of bark-covered tree limbs. He stripped off the bark, placed it on the paper, lighted and blew it into a small flame. Patience and the addition of small, then larger branches resulted in enough heat so Patti could shrug out of her jacket.

She found a decrepit broom, gritted her teeth, and began brushing cobwebs and spider webs from the ceiling and walls.

"Spiders, start packin'. This place ain't

big enough for both of us, and I ain't leavin'," she announced in a passable imitation of John Wayne's drawl. She was delighted at Scott's hearty laugh. Her spirits rose a notch. This interlude in an isolated mountain cabin would be something to tell their children and grandchildren. Patti pounced on an aged water bucket, then a large shallow pan perfect for heating water. She felt she had struck gold.

"If you'll bring me some water, I can heat it and start scrubbing this place while you bring in more wood," she suggested.

"Right. You're the best sport in the world, Patti," he praised.

She caught the admiration in his face and bit her tongue. Even though she didn't deserve his approval, telling him otherwise wouldn't help their situation. She peered out the narrow crack where Scott had left the door open to air out the place. "Maybe I should come with you. It's starting to snow harder."

"I'll be better off without you."

"Thanks a lot," Patti retorted, although she knew he was right. "Run along then, water boy. You're holding up progress." Again his laughter raised her spirits. It also gave her a foretaste of the strength Scott would show throughout their life together.

Anyone who could laugh while stranded miles from civilization would certainly wear well. Patti whispered a little prayer to be worthy of his love and went back to her cleaning.

By nightfall, the inside of Charley's Folly had been relieved of as many layers of grime as they could manage. After a meager meal, Patti and Scott gratefully seated themselves on the chairs, taking care not to make any sudden moves. She rubbed her aching back and looked around in satisfaction. The Folly even smelled clean. She and Scott had disposed of grimy blankets and dead boughs. Repeated sweepings, then mopping with stream water heated on the iron stove, had cleansed the floor enough so Scott could sleep there. Best of all, no spider could possibly have withstood the cleaning onslaught.

"Still a far cry from a Hilton," she said. "But a whole lot better than before."

"You're a pioneer in denim," Scott teased. The love in his dark eyes warmed Patti. Nothing in his lean face warranted the nickname Stone Face now.

"*Pioneer in Denim* would make a good book title," Patti mused. Her eyes half closed, then popped open. Her fingers itched for pencil or brush. "Scott, I want to paint pictures of this place when I get back. I'll call them 'Before and After.' "

He squeezed her hand, then dropped it. "I've seen some of your work, Patti. You can do it. If not now, later." He abruptly broke off.

Patti felt his spirit had retreated to a place where she could not follow. Surely he didn't regret telling her he cared! Yet what else would darken his eyes and bring the old brooding look back?

"What is it?" she whispered.

"I'm trying to figure out the right way to deal with Charles Bradley."

She straightened. The prehistoric chair creaked a warning and she gingerly sagged back against it.

"Do? Force him to admit the truth, of course. Isn't it what you've waited for all these years?" Patti's indignant words tumbled into the room like kittens at play chasing one another.

"Yes." He stared at his clenched hands, then looked at her beseechingly. "When I heard Bradley mumbling, I could barely wait to use his confession to set the record straight. I asked the passenger who overheard to remember, so he could be my witness. Yet ever since the crash, it doesn't seem important. I keep thinking how Jesus preached forgiveness and practiced it even on the cross."

Scott's troubled gaze never left Patti's face.

"Charles Bradley is washed up as a pilot. Why kick him when he's down? Rehashing the past will also bring everything back to the families of the men who died. It just isn't worth it."

Patti took his strong hands in her smaller ones, rough from scrubbing.

"If I hadn't already loved you more than anything in this world except God, I'd fall in love with you now," she fiercely told him. "Scott Sloan, I'm so proud of you I could cry, but I won't!" She blinked back the flood just behind her eyes.

"Do you really mean it?" Scott whispered. He stood and put his arms around her. "What about the way Bradley treated you? Are you sure you won't always secretly feel I let you down by not retaliating?"

Patti buried her face against his chest and shook her head. "I will always feel you did what Jesus would do," she whispered. She felt the tempo of his steady heartbeat quicken. Her own unpleasantness with Charles seemed long ago and far away, as if it had happened to a totally different person. Perhaps it had. The last two days' ordeal had irrevocably changed both Scott and her. Because of God's great mercy, turning the other cheek had become a privilege, not a chore.

A day of light snow followed that adventurous day, then another day of fog. Food supplies ran low.

"Why couldn't we have ended up in this predicament when there were berries for food?" Patti privately asked God. "Our rations won't carry us much longer. We need Your help, Lord." She knew Scott felt the same by his set expression. He had tried to catch a fish, but the venture proved unsuccessful.

Late in the afternoon of the third day at the Charley's Folly Hilton, Scott hiked down to the stream for fresh water. Patti watched him fill the canteens and sling them over his shoulders. He filled the bucket and started back. Two-thirds of the way up the trail, he stumbled over a hidden rock and knocked it loose. The snow-softened earth loosened and moved beneath his boots.

"Look out!" Patti screamed. She raced down the upper part of the trail, heedless of her own safety.

"Go back!" Scott yelled. The bucket of

water went flying. The canteens jounced against his body. A mighty leap forward landed him on solid ground. He grabbed Patti's arm and raced with her to safety. A horrid rumbling sounded.

They whipped around. The place where Scott had stood moments before no longer existed. A ragged break in the earth a few feet below them marked where the trail had been before Scott inadvertently triggered the avalanche.

Patti clung to his arm. "You could be down there!" she choked.

"I'm not, but the water is." He shut his lips tightly.

Patti sensed he regretted pointing out the obvious.

"We can always melt and purify snow," she reminded. "Besides, it's starting to clear." She pointed west.

"So it is." He relaxed. "If it stays like this, help will come tomorrow."

Patti rejoiced and followed him back to the shack. When they got inside Scott said, "When the chopper arrives, you're going to have another new experience."

"Is that a promise or a threat?" she asked, hoping to make him smile.

He didn't respond to her teasing. "A little of both. There's no place up here by the shack for a chopper to set down. We can't climb back down to the crash site. After what happened today, no way are we climbing on up to the top of the canyon. That means we'll have to be airlifted out of here."

Patti felt as if the wind had been knocked from her. "You mean like on TV?"

"Exactly." A teasing expression came into his face. "I'll stay on the ground and catch you if you fall."

Bang! Patti's attempts to be a good sport popped like a taut balloon.

"That isn't funny, Scott."

"I'm sorry. It was a fool thing to say. You'll be perfectly safe." He wrapped his arms around her and held her until most of her fear evaporated. Scott would never lie to her. If he said being airlifted from the ground to a helicopter was safe, she had no need to worry.

The next morning, Patti licked dry lips and tried to smile while Scott got her into the harness that had been lowered from the Bell Jet-Ranger. Mike Parker was at the controls. Patti realized he must have checked out their situation, for he hovered a safe distance above them while a second man worked the airlift. Patti followed Scott's advice, "Don't look down if it bothers you," until he called, "Take her up." She felt herself lifted from the ground. Heart in throat, she risked a quick glance then concentrated on being drawn up and up, and into the chopper.

"Fancy meeting you here," she managed to get out between her clenched teeth.

Both pilots roared at her inane remark. "Now for Stone Face," Mike said. Down went the harness. Up came Scott, carrying her medical bag and the badly depleted survival pack. No use in leaving its contents. The avalanche had made access to Charley's Folly next to impossible.

"Thanks for rescuing me and my fiancée," he said easily. His broad grin set Patti's pulses racing.

"About time," Mike Parker chortled. "Let's go home. There's a couple of surprises waiting for you in Kalispell. Want to hear them now or later?"

"Later," Scott replied. "We've had enough surprises."

"Okay. Just remember. I tried to warn you." Mike chuckled.

Patti wondered what he meant by the cryptic remark. She was too tired to care. Out of danger, all she wanted to do was sleep and . . .

"You don't happen to have a steak up your sleeve, do you?" she mumbled.

"No, but we brought sandwiches and hot soup." The copilot passed them back. Patti hadn't known ham and cheese on sourdough bread could taste so good. By the time she finished eating, Charley's Folly, even the helicopter crash, seemed a lifetime ago. She fell asleep with her head on Scott's shoulder.

"Reporters. Great. Just what we don't need."

Scott's disgusted comment awakened Patti. Mike had set the helicopter down at the flying field. Camera crews and reporters raced across the tarmac.

"Hey, Sloan, how does it feel to be a hero?" one shrilled. Other questions followed.

Mike Parker leaped from the chopper. His bellow cut off the babble. "Pilot and nurse are fine, but it's been rough out there. Go ahead and take your pictures, but I'll do the talking. Otherwise, I'll have you thrown in the hoosegow for trespassing on private property." His grin didn't hide that he meant it.

Patti didn't learn what had happened in her absence until the next day. The Hoffs returned Obsidian from the Running H. They had taken him home with them the first night Patti spent on the mountain.

"Land sakes, but we were worried," Ma confessed. "Then the paper came out and —"

"The paper?" Patti's brain still felt tired after hours and hours of sleep.

"Yes." Satisfaction oozed from her voice. "I cut out the story."

Patti stared at the headlines.

PILOT SCOTT SLOAN CLEARED OF OLD
CHARGES
AFTER RESCUING INJURED PLANE CRASH
SURVIVORS.

The well-written story played up the bizarre twist to the rescue of Charles Bradley and his three passengers. Evidently the youngest passenger had wasted no time in exposing Charles's inexcusable conduct in flying after drinking, along with the facts that came out on the helicopter flight back to Kalispell.

That evening, Scott, Patti, and Obsidian sat in front of a blazing fire — a family, soon to be together forever with God as head of the household.

"The Lord was in control all the time I agonized about Charles," Scott said.

"It doesn't lessen the worth of your decision," Patti reminded him. "You had no way of knowing what God had planned for the future."

"I know." Scott's fingers strayed to his shirt pocket. He slowly took out a sealed envelope. "Neither did Dan Davis, but he gave this to Mike Parker shortly after you brought him home from Seattle, with specific orders about delivery."

Patti stared at her and Scott's scrawled names, followed by the words: "To be opened together."

"I don't understand."

"I don't either, Darling. Open it."

Why should her fingers tremble? Had Dan changed his mind at the last minute and made a will in favor of Scott? Was her inheritance to be snatched away? Patti hated herself for the selfish thought. Scott's or hers, it didn't matter.

She spread out the single page and read it aloud.

If you receive this letter, it means God has seen fit to grant an old man's wish. Patti, you're the daughter I never had. Only one man I know is good enough for you: Scott Sloan. That's part of the reason I'm leaving you my property. If you're here for a time, perhaps you will learn to know and love my friend Scott. If not, you'll never be troubled by an old man's foolishness. God bless and keep you, second Sarah.

Patti's heart overflowed. She slipped into her beloved's arms and silently thanked God for His love and Scott's: warm, lasting, and radiant enough to surpass even the orange and scarlet reflection of glowing promises dancing on the hearth of her log cabin home.

ABOUT THE AUTHOR

Colleen L. Reece learned to read beneath the rays of a kerosene lamp. The kitchen, dining room, and her bedroom in her home near the small logging town of Darrington, Washington, were once a one-room schoolhouse where her mother taught all eight grades!

An abundance of love for God and for each other outweighed the lack of electricity or running water and provided the basis for many of Colleen's 135 books. Her rigid "refuse to compromise" stance has helped sell more than 3 million copies that spread the good news of repentance, forgiveness, and salvation through Christ.

Colleen helped launch Barbour Publishing's Romance Reader flip books and the American Adventure series and had her own Juli Scott Super Sleuth Christian teen mystery series. Colleen is most well-known for helping to launch Heartsong Presents in

1992, for which she had been awarded Favorite Author in numerous Reader's Polls. In 1998, Colleen was inducted into the Heartsong Hall of Fame in recognition for her contribution to Heartsong's success.

The first two titles in this series of "Seattle" stories was first written for Heartsong Presents under Colleen's pen name of Connie Loraine.

Her personal creed: simply to help make the world a better place because she lived it.